BENEATH HIM

Beneath Him

C. SHELL

C. Shell

Beneath Him

by
C. Shell
Harlow Book One

Table of Contents

Beneath Him

Copyright

Dedication

This book is dedicated to those who enjoy a book with a tough heroine and a male that never gives up and gives zero fucks about what is considered proper and right. If you prefer to color outside of the lines then this book is for you.

PRAISE FOR AUTHOR

C. Shell AND HER BOOKS

"Very good book! Alex is domineering, possessive and sexy. Jessica is a normal, sweet woman with trust issues when it comes to rich men. Can't wait to read the next book."

-Jenee's Book Blog

~*~

"...a steamy story which includes a strong-minded, bull-headed girl that falls for a hot, sexy and gorgeous alpha...warning, there's a cliff hanger and I can't wait to read the next installment."

~Angela's Sizzling Pages

Chapter One

"Jessica, please say yes!"

My roommate Jane is worse than a dog with a bone when she wants something, and today is no different. Whenever she calls me by my full name instead of my nickname, *Jess*, she means business.

She has been driving me crazy for over an hour, begging me to take over her job today, as the head makeup artist for a photo shoot at *Glimmer Magazine*. Under normal circumstances, I would jump at the opportunity. *Glimmer Magazine* is one of the top five women's fashion magazines in the country and currently one of our finest clients.

With the idea that I would be off work today, I went out last night with a few friends to check out the stylish new club that recently opened down the street. After one too many drinks and lots of dancing, we stayed until the place closed their doors and kicked us out. I'm regretting that decision today. My head feels like someone put it through a meat grinder.

Leaning over my bathroom counter, I apply new tea bags to my eyes and pray the beauty gods have mercy on me by reducing the puffiness and redness from my eyes. If I tried, I'm sure I could wring alcohol out of my skin. That is how much I consumed last night.

Never again. I have to remember I'm not a fish and, therefore, can't drink like one.

Stomping back into my room, Jane is determined to win me over. As always, I'll end up giving in to her. I normally do, but to feed my own sick amusement, I'll make her work for it by groveling a little more. That is what friends are for, right?

She and I have been friends since our freshman year of college. We both majored as Makeup Artist/Specialists, so right away we had a lot in common, and later became room-mates as well.

To say her parents are well off is putting it mildly. I'm not joking around. Her parents are loaded down with homes and condos sprinkled around the globe. They are also down to earth and the sweetest people you will ever meet. After we graduated, they offered their lavish condo in Dallas to us for free until our business gets more established and we can save up enough money to get a place of our own.

My family has never been close like Jane's are. Over the years, her parents have unofficially adopted me as their own. I don't know what I would have done, or where I would have ended up if Jane hadn't wandered into my life.

"Please, Jessica! I will owe you big time. This weekend is my only chance to spend time with David before he leaves for Germany for a whole month."

Rolling my eyes for emphasis, I let her off the hook and nod my head in agreement. "Fine. I will step in and work the shoot for you today. Don't think I'll forget. I have every intention on cashing in this favor in the future."

Screeching with happiness, Jane leaps at me, hugging me tightly, and almost knocking me on my ass in the process. I grimace at her enthusiasm. "Thank me quieter, please,"

I beg. "My head can't take loud noises right now." With gentle precision, I rub tiny circles at my temples, trying to ease the pain slicing through them.

"Sorry, I forgot. Wait right here. I have the perfect thing for your hangover."

"Unless it requires bullets, I'm not sure it will help," I tease.

Jane rushes back into my bathroom holding out two Tylenol and a warm cup of tea sweetened with honey. "Take these and drink all of this," she says, pushing the cup into my outstretched hand. "You will be better within an hour. I promise."

Not that I don't trust my friend, but I have tried her *foolproof* plans before, and they always leave me worse off than I started. With the day ticking by and my appointment on the horizon, I don't have time to argue. Taking a risk, I gulp down the pills, and honey-flavored tea before heading off towards the shower.

The hot water is just what I needed to help wash away my aches and the fallout from my night out. Once clean, I dress quickly in a deep-green cashmere summer sweater paired with skinny black jeans and my new, black, stiletto, leather boots.

The delicious smell of coffee wafting in from the kitchen calls to me like a druggy needing his next fix. Not one to turn down caffeine, I make a small deter from the tasks of getting ready and stalk into the other room in search of a cup of Joe. Jane smiles at me knowingly as she hands me a cup already filled to the brim and lightened with the perfect amounts of cream and sugar. Just the way I like it. This is why I love her. She knows me better than anyone and takes care of me like family.

I smile up at her as I take a tentative sip, being careful not to burn my tongue. "This coffee tastes excellent. If you were a man I would snatch you up in a heartbeat," I giggle.

"I know, and I appreciate it, Jess. Come sit with me and I'll explain about today's shoot. It's not much different from others we've done, but you'll be by yourself on this one so make sure you prepare and bring everything with you."

Following her over to our overstuffed sofa, I curl into the opposite corner from her and tuck my feet under me as I get comfortable. "I remember the contract said something about an article being done on highly sought after eligible men from Dallas. Right?" I don't always see every contract that comes into the office, but the larger ones always catch my eye.

"That's the gist of it," she agrees with a smile. "The spread they're doing will be centered on five wealthy men. It should be an easy job since you won't have to deal with any drama queen mommas. Make-up will be minimal, and the shoot should take no longer than four hours. I'll text you the address so you can download it into your GPS."

"Sounds easy enough." I glance back at the clock with a sigh, making sure I have sufficient time to finish getting ready before I need to leave. I'm neurotic when it comes to being on time for a job.

"I'm going to finish putting my face on and do something to fix this mop of hair on my head," I say, with a wave of my hand. "So, where are you and David going this weekend?"

"He is taking me to his parent's vacation house on Lake Travis for two nights. If our plans hold true, we will be partying our asses off down on Sixth Street, in Austin. We've been so busy lately with work that I feel like we never see enough of each other. I plan to use this weekend to remind that man why he loves me," she squeals.

"I hope David realizes what a lucky bastard he is. He doesn't deserve you," I call out, on my way back to my room.

I like David well enough, but I don't think he is good enough for Jane. She has the kindest heart and would do anything for a friend in need. David is always pleasant to Jane, but he consistently takes advantage of her good nature. I secretly think he keeps her around just so he can have a smoking hot girl on his arm.

Jane is the average height of five-foot-six inches with killer legs, a natural tan that most girls pay top dollar for, long, golden blonde hair, skinny as a rail, and baby-blue eyes. She is a living Barbie and a walking dirty dream.

She and I are opposites. If we were cars, then she would be a sleek Porsche and I would be a trusty Ford truck. Not that I'm ugly or anything, but I would never make it into the Barbie Hall of Fame. Not unless they decide to make a short Barbie with pale skin, a thin but curvy figure, wavy brown hair, and boring brown eyes. Nope, Barbie would not know what to do with hips and breasts larger than a size B, although I bet money Ken would not mind them.

Running my hands through my hair, I opt to throw it on top of my head in a stylish, but simple bun with a few tendrils shadowing my face. There is nothing worse than trying to work with a client while having your hair fall in your face every time you bend over. Now for some black mascara, a little blush, and a splash of pink lip gloss. Voila, I am ready to go. Taking one last look in the mirror, I'm pleasantly stunned that after the wild night I had, I've managed to clean up quite nicely.

I look pretty damn good.

Checking the clock, I frown; I have no time to spare. *Damn, I hate being rushed.* Now if only my feet would stop hurting. I haven't even left our apartment yet, and my feet are already protesting my choice in footwear. Thank heavens this gig is short. If it lasts longer than a few hours, I might be needing someone to carry me to my car by the end of the day.

Reminder to self: new leather shoes need breaking in before wearing them out.

No time for that now. Grabbing my purse, keys, and cell phone, I kiss Jane goodbye while making her promise to contact me once she arrives at the lake house. Not that I don't trust David, but I won't be able to relax tonight until I know she arrived and everything is going okay.

Jumping into my little, red, convertible Mazda that purrs like a happy kitten, I zip down freeway 161 toward the north side of town. Blaring my radio, I sing along to Britney Spears song "Womanizer" as I enjoy the lack of traffic and the cool wind on my face. Pulling into *Glimmer Magazine*, I show my credentials to a gruff-looking guard who, despite my many attempts at a few jokes, refuses to crack a smile or give a simple pity laugh. Plastering on a fake smile, I thank him for his time and follow his directions to a sectioned off parking area near the front doors.

I rush inside the building and take the first bank of elevators I find up to the thirteenth floor. I've never worked a shoot for this magazine before. Jane has always been the one to handle this account and has never come back with a bad review.

The Harlow family owns this magazine, along with a few smaller, side businesses. The publication was founded by the late Mrs. Jocelyn Harlow. She passed away four years ago from cancer and left everything to her only son Alex Harlow. Since becoming CEO at the ripe old age of twenty-four, he has taken an already profitable business and tripled its readership and sales in record time. Rumor has it he is worth millions. Plagued by curiosity, I tried Googling him to find a current photo of him but came back with nothing. Besides a handful of business reports and short, nondescript biographies, the man is a ghost.

As the elevator doors spring open, my eyes sweep over the room, and my jaw hangs in awe. I've never seen anything like this. The whole floor is one huge studio that's sole purpose is for taking photos for the magazine. *My own little piece of heaven.*

The ceilings are high and go on forever with track lighting blanketing the whole area. You can easily run seven photo shoots at the same time in here. My favorite part is a secluded section in the back of the studio that houses an assortment of backdrops, props, and every type of camera you could ever dream of having. The place is fantastic and well thought out.

Before I left the apartment, Jane told me to search out a short, brown-haired, plump lady named Kelly. She supposedly will be the one to instruct me on where to set up and give me my schedule for the day. Gazing into the sea of bodies scurrying around, I begin to panic. How in the hell am I to find one person out of the hundreds running around?

I'm not normally a nervous person, but I'm out of my element here surrounded by all these strangers. After ten minutes of mindless searching, I have yet to find this so called Kelly person. As my mother always says, when in doubt ask someone.

Scanning the area, I decide to ask a small man standing beside the snack table who reminds me of a little garden gnome. His hideous, dark purple pantsuit, kind face, and headset attached to his balding head make him a safe choice.

"Excuse me, sir. Do you know where I could find Kelly?" I internally cringe at how screechy my voice comes across. The man jumps and I have to bite back a giggle as his lop-sided smile and wide eyes land on me.

Answering around the gooey donut stuffed in his mouth, he spurts, "She is the brunette standing over by James. He is the photographer." He points to the far wall behind him. "Over there near those guys in the suits."

Following the direction of his extended finger, I find my target. I give him a small smile as I eye the yummy-looking donut in his chubby fingers. "Thanks for your help."

Thank goodness I arrived early or else I would be late, and late is a four-letter word in my vocabulary. I make haste across the studio while trying not to bump into anyone on my way to greet the infamous Kelly.

Skidding to a stop behind her, I reach forward and tap lightly on her shoulder. "Excuse me, Kelly. My name is Jessica Grayson. I'm filling in as the make-up artist for Jane Tillson today on the local bachelor set." I'm proud of how professional my voice sounds despite my frayed nerves.

She glares at me. Her abrasive eyes take me in as if I'm nothing more than a piece of gum stuck to the bottom of her favorite shoes. I gulp, instinctively knowing that, for whatever reason, this lady does not like me. My stomach twists into knots, similar to the way it used to back when

I was in grade school and sent to the principal's office for being bad. Not that I was in trouble often, but there were a few times when my mouth would respond faster than my brain.

"It's about time you showed up. You were on the cusp of being fired. We do not tolerate tardiness," she hisses, turning her back on me. "Follow me, please, and I will show you to your station. James here will be the photographer on the set you're working."

My brows rise in confusion as I look down and check my watch. "The contract said noon," I muse. "I'm right on time."

Kelly ignores my rebuttal and continues with her previous conversation with the man now known as James. Gripping him by the arm, she turns and begins walking away. Not wanting to be left behind and piss her off more than I already have, I follow, walking faster than my sore feet can tolerate in order to keep up.

We stop in front of a desk with a full-length mirror in the back, far corner of the studio. With a wave of her hand, Kelly announces this will be my station. The area is small, but the lighting here is amazing.

"You have five minutes to prepare before we begin sending people to your station. You're allowed only fifteen minutes to prep them before each shoot. Each gentleman will be included in two sets of shots today." Handing me a list of names she continues, "The men will arrive in this order. Keep up, or you and I will have a problem. And last but not least, remember that you're being paid to make our inteviwrs look good, not to be their new best friend or future girlfriend."

I blink, shocked and taken off guard by her words. *Bitchy much?* Looking her straight in the eye, I nod my understanding. I refuse to let this overworked bitsy talk down to me as though I'm an irresponsible child who has no control over her hormones.

"Not a problem. I am nothing if not professional. No worries here. I will be ready on time and won't slow any-one down." I give her a polite smile while imagining the feel of my hand making contact with her snarky face. "Thanks again for contacting our company, and I hope you have a great day, Kelly."

****

Setup was a breeze, and the first two needed very little touching up. At this rate, I should be out of here within three hour's tops. I'm ready to go home, veg out on my sofa, and watch the latest episode of *Grey's Anatomy* on my DVR.

Why can't I ever meet a doctor like that McDreamy character?

I glance at my watch. I have four minutes before Deacon is set to arrive in my chair for a little powdering. My break-fast of only coffee does not agree with my ravenous appe-tite. My stomach won't stop growling. I know I promised to be good and not leave my station, but I feel the need to break the rules a little. Running to steal a donut off the snack table before Deacon arrives isn't being all that naughty, is it? It might not be the definition of professional in Kelly's world, but neither is having your stomach growl-ing for everyone who gets within five feet of you.

I am getting that damn donut!

Donut in hand, I sprint back from the snack table and manage to trip over my own feet. Arms flying, donut fall-ing, and legs buckling, I lose my balance and head straight toward the polished floor. Mere inches from a hard and un-forgiving face plant, which would no doubt hurt like hell,

I'm rescued as an arm snakes out and catches me mid-fall. Mr. Strong Arms straightens to his full height, taking me with him, as his hand keeps an iron grip on my arm. The heat from his touch sends a warm and unwelcome shiver down my spine.

"Sorry for running into you," I say breathlessly while trying to get a clear look at my rescuer. My back is plastered to his chest, and the way he's gripping my arm, I can't turn my head enough to see him.

When he doesn't respond right away, I keep talking. "I was in a hurry to get back to my station and apparently wasn't paying attention to the wires on the floor. I promise to do a better job of watching where I'm going in the future."

Bending down, I grab my ruined donut off the floor, using the napkin wrapped around it to wipe up any fallen crumbs. My lips twist into a frown seeing bits of dirt stuck to the brightly glazed top. *What a waste of a good donut.*

I try to step away but Mr. Strong Arms has yet to release his hold on me. In fact, if anything, his grip has tightened. I glance up, ready to protest, only to find myself staring into the most beautiful, intense, and angry green eyes I've ever seen.

Chapter Two

Why is he angry?

I don't understand why this beautiful man before me looks as though he wants to stomp me into the ground. I've already apologized for running into him, and yet his jaw is clenched so tight, I'm afraid he might break off some of his teeth.

I know it's rude to stare, but I can't look away. It feels as though my eyes are glued to his. He is perfect in every capacity, from his raven-black hair, severe emerald-green eyes, on down to his chiseled Abercrombie features, and hard as steel torso. His expensive dark suit and pale-blue shirt stand out among the casually dressed crew of photographers, lighting techs, and other common workers around here.

Although he's handsome enough to be one of the many models standing about, I immediately dismiss that notion. This man is way too domineering and significant to be a model. He apparently doesn't work on this floor, so that means he must be in the marketing department, or perhaps higher up, like a management position or one of the many legal guys.

Jane would describe him as panty-drop gorgeous. *I would have to agree.*

His lips twitch as his eyes flick down to my lips. Warmth spreads through my belly and I light up like a circuit board. Even clothed, you can tell he's built like a god. What would it feel like to be with a man like him? Writhing beneath him while he brings me to orgasm. My face heats as a small moan escapes my lips, and I quickly duck my head in embarrassed at my overactive imagination.

Lord, I need to get laid.

I shake myself out of my lust-filled daze, coming back to the present and the problem at hand. I struggle to find my voice, which is crazy because no man has ever rendered me speechless before. I hate to break my connection with him, but I can't afford to screw this job up any more than I already have.

"Could you please let go of my arm? I need to get back to my area before I cause the photographer any grief. You have no idea how bad that would be for me today," I say, my voice soft.

He is quick to drop my arm, acting as though it burned him. Then, without saying a single word, he turns and storms off toward the elevators. I stare at my arm where he was holding it with a frown. I immediately miss the warmth of his touch. He is by far the most beautiful and confusing creature I have ever met.

I don't have time to contemplate why or how I upset him or even why I reacted to him the way I did. I need to get back to my booth before anyone realizes I've left. Sprinting back down the way I came, I arrive just as a very red-faced and pissed off James walks up.

Great! Now I get to deal with another aggravated man, and on top of everything, my stomach is still growling from hunger.

"James, I am truly sorry. If I…"

He cuts me off before I can finish, and the yelling ensues. "Ms. Grayson, you promised to stay on top of things today, and yet, here I am, waiting on Deacon." He glances over at Deacon who is leaning against the outer wall as if he has no care in the world. James's face heats to a bright red. "You haven't even started on his make-up! What is the holdup?"

Swallowing the lump lodged in my throat, I try once again to explain, knowing it won't help. I don't think there is anything I could say to undo the damage done. In his eyes I am a nothing but a lost case that is taking up his precious time.

My eyes tear up as I speak. "James, I am sincerely sorry. I had four minutes before Deacon was to arrive, and in my haste to get to work this morning, I overlooked eating breakfast. My stomach was upset, so I went to grab a quick bite to eat with the assumption that I could make it back before I would be needed again. On the way here I ran into someone, and everything went wrong after that."

I stand before him wringing my hands together and rambling like a fool. With his face a few shades redder than before, he throws his arms in the air to emphasize his exasperation with me as he lets out a low growl.

Jane fucking owes me, big time. First, a hangover from hell and now this. I should have stayed in bed today.

"Please," he huffs through clenched teeth. "Just stop your yapping and get Deacon ready so we can finish up before the next crew needs this set. No more unscheduled breaks, Ms. Grayson," he barks.

The next three hours go by in a haze. Luckily, this shoot is easy and does not require much consideration. My body is working on autopilot while my mind is spinning with indecent images centered on the mysterious man I ran into earlier. I can't believe I forgot to get his name, not that he seemed inclined to give it. I have had several boyfriends and one serious relationship, but never has a man affected me the way he did. With a simple touch, he had my body humming and begging for more. My lack of sex must've made me starved for male attention. That is the only reasonable explanation I can come up with that makes sense.

My dry spell is catching up with me.

Throwing the last tube of primer into my kit, I wipe off the counter and trace my steps back toward the bank of elevators. With tense muscles and achy feet, I'm ready to get home and soak in a hot bath.

Leaning against the back wall waiting for the elevator car, I'm taken off guard as a distraught Kelly comes flying around the corner, yelling out my name like a banshee.

"Ms. Grayson! I'm so glad to have caught you before you left. Mr. Harlow would like to have a word with you. He's waiting for you in his office on the twentieth floor."

My mouth drops open, gaping like a fish out of the water. Flabbergasted, my mood started to sink at the thought of being in trouble. "I'm...I'm sorry. I don't understand. Why does Mr. Harlow wish to speak with me?"

This can't be good. Jane is going to kill me if I screwed up this job.

"It is not my job to question the boss's orders, Ms. Grayson. I only follow them," she deadpans. As the elevator doors open, she scoots me inside, presses the button for the twentieth floor and gives me a weak smile.

As the elevator descends, I make a quick assessment of my attire and fixed the few tendrils of hair that has fallen out in the course of the day. My mind is racing with *what ifs* and *whys*. The only possible reason I can come up with as to why Mr. Harlow is asking for me would be because of James.

I'm guessing he complained about me for slowing down his precious shoot. Jane and I haven't been in business together very long, and a complaint about us from a prominent magazine like *Glimmer* would be the final nail in our career coffins.

Dallas might seem like a large city, but it feels minuscule for people in our profession. Once the rumors take flight, we'll be knocked straight on our asses. My hands are unsteady; despite my best effort, I can't stop them from shaking.

As the doors open, I exit the elevators into a large, open reception area. Overly large cream-colored, leather couches and chairs span one side of the room with ornate iron tables laid among them. The place oozes sophistication and class. I hesitantly walk up to a large mahogany desk where a small, older lady sits, typing eagerly on her computer. She doesn't seem to notice me as I approach her, but she is the only other person around, so obviously she must be his receptionist.

"Excuse me," I say, catching her attention. "My name is Jessica Grayson. Kelly told me Mr. Harlow requested to see me." My voice is as shaky as my hands. I clear my throat in an effort to control my emotions.

She glances up and me with a warm inviting smile. "Mr. Harlow had to go handle something for a moment. Please wait for him in his office. He will be with you shortly." Standing, she motions for me to follow her down a large hallway that ends at two large, heavy, wooden doors. I follow her in and promptly decline when she inquires if I'd like anything to drink.

I would love a stiff drink right now, but I have a feeling that would only hamper my situation.

The room is decorated in the same manner as the reception area, with overly large, leather seating and dark, wooden furniture. I'm stunned by the ample size of the room. The entire back wall is floor to ceiling glass that reflects upon the greater Dallas area. The view is truly spectacular.

Taking a seat in one of the chairs across from his desk, I contemplate how I'm going talk my way out of this. Surely, I won't be tossed out on my ass for one minor mistake...right? Dwelling on the problem at hand, my head snaps at the sound of the door opening.

My eyes widen. "What the hell?" I squeak as my voice rises several unflattering octaves. Surprise takes me as I find myself once again staring into the glorious, green eyes that belong to my mysterious savior from earlier.

"You have got to be kidding me. I can't believe you tattled on me," I shout. "It was a simple mistake, buddy." My voice is unsteady as I try and hold in my anger. "I've already apologized for running into you. What else do you want, my first born?" I run my hands through my hair to keep from strangling the confusing and gorgeous man standing before me. His knowing smirk is not helping matters.

I'm defenseless against him. This is insane. I am lusting after a man who could ruin me and cause me to lose one of our largest clients.

Clearing his throat, the man finally speaks. Damn if he does not have the sexiest, profound and gravelly voice I've ever had the pleasure of hearing.

"You don't sound very sorry, Ms. Grayson," he says, folding himself into the empty seat beside mine.

The man is infuriating, to say the least. "I was sincerely sorry at the time, but I must admit, knowing you tattled on me doesn't make me the least bit apologetic anymore. It was an innocent mistake, and judging by the fact that you are walking fine and do not appear hurt, I would have to say no harm was done."

He laughs out loud. The deep sound hits me straight between my legs, causing me to squeeze them together in hopes of easing the warmth gathering there.

"You are a feisty one, aren't you?"

"No. Not generally," I murmur under my breath. I fidget as I feel his eyes on me. "I am at a disadvantage. You clearly have learned my name, but you never did tell me yours."

Curiosity is eating at me. I want to know the name of this beautiful asshat!

The tension between us thickens as he leans in close. His scent of fresh cinnamon and vanilla envelopes me, giving me a natural high that is all him. He smells divine, not that I would expect anything less. Taking my hand in his, he lightly kisses the tops of my knuckles, sending jolts of electricity through my body. My brows dip as I stare up at him in complete awe.

What the hell is going on?

"Please forgive my bad manners, Ms. Grayson. My name is Alex Harlow, but you may call me Alex, sir, or my all-time favorite, Master of the Universe," he says, a sly smile tainting his lips.

"Fuck me," I breathe, feeling as if someone has just knocked the wind out of me.

Chapter Three

Shit. Fuck. Screw a monkey.

Please let this be a bad dream. I blink multiple times, but it is no use. No matter how many times I re-open my eyes, the same horrible scene lays before me. How did I not see this before? I've got to do better research on who my clients are...even if they are thrown at me at the last minute.

Hell will freeze over before I ever call him *Master of the Universe!* I bite back the urge to slap that smug look right off his face. I straighten my shoulders and refuse to let this pompous, self-righteous man get the best of me. "Mr. Harlow, would you please enlighten me as to why you had me brought to your office?"

Ignoring my question, he stands and moves to the wet bar in the corner and proceeds to pour himself a stiff drink of what appears to be bourbon. Glancing back at me he inquires," Would you care to join me in a drink, Jessica?"

Rolling my eyes in irritation, I shake my head no. This man is intoxicating enough without liquor added to the mix. I need to keep all my wits about me while around him. "I appreciate the offer, but no, and please, call me Ms. Grayson."

He chuckles. While he enjoys his drink, I cautiously allow my eyes to rove over his spectacular physique. Broad shoulders, a muscular yet lean body, and a face that should be in a magazine instead of behind it is what I register before he sits his glass down and retakes the chair beside me.

What is his game? He is very powerful, and I have no doubt he never does anything without an agenda, so what is his end game with me?

Stretching out his long legs as he leans comfortably back in his seat, he glances up at me, and I'm immediately lost in his jade eyes, all dark and serious. His hand reaches over and covers mine as his thumb gently strokes small circles over my knuckles. Why does he keep touching me? I want to ask, but I can't breathe, let alone speak.

Get it together, Jess. This man is out of your league and will eat you alive.

The sexual tension is so thick in the room you could cut it with a knife. I pull my hand back into my lap and give my head a shake, trying unsuccessfully to clear my muddled musings. "Mr. Harlow, as I asked before, why did you have me brought to your office? If this is about my job performance today, then please speak up. Otherwise, it's getting late, and I should be heading home."

His eyes darken as they lock with my own. "Have dinner with me tonight, Jessica." He is not asking as much as telling me.

I think I could use that drink about now.

"Excuse me? I was under the assumption that I'm here because I ran into you today which forced the set to go longer than planned?"

"Yes, that was unfortunate, but I'm not such a hard-ass that I would hold that over your head. Although, in the future you should eat before coming to work. Breakfast is important," he reprimands, his lips turning down with a frown.

I want to laugh, but instead hold my tongue. I can't believe he is scolding me like a misbehaving child. He doesn't know me and yet, he's more concerned over my dietary needs than my mother has ever been. I need to get out of here before I say something I'll regret. Mr. Harlow is pure trouble with a capital T. He oozes enough sex appeal to drive a nun to orgasm.

"Jessica, you haven't answered me about dinner," he chides. His harsh tone doesn't sit well with me. "What would you like to eat? There is a new Japanese restaurant not far from here. The reviews on it have been marvelous. I do believe that is your favorite food, is it not?"

I huff in silence as my mind and body battle for dominance. This man is insane and too confident for his own good, and yet, he is delicious to look at. *How in God's name does he know what my favorite cuisine is?* Has he been checking up on me? Dinner is out of the question. He's a client, and I don't mix businesses with pleasure. As my mind screams, "No," my body is begging me to say, "Yes."

"My food preference is none of your concern, Mr. Harlow," I counter. I clasp my hands tighter as I try to ease the slight tremble in them. "I find it a bit disconcerting that you would know anything personal about me. That seems a bit, I don't know..." I pause, searching for the right word. When it comes to me, I say it with a rigid smile, "Stalkerish."

Mr. Harlow laughs, the sound once again wrapping around me and turning my insides to mush.

"No stalking needed. It's amazing what you can learn about a person from social media. Everything posted on there is public knowledge and being a good boss ensures that I know everything I can about my employees."

Staring at the closed door behind him, I decide to end this discussion before it can get any worse. "I appreciate the offer for dinner, but I do not like to mix work with pleasure, so I must decline."

He gives me a don't-be-stupid stare that has me itching to run out the door and never look back. Leaning forward, with his elbows propped on his knees, he looks through me. Not at me, but through me, as if he can see all my secrets and desires. I fidget in response.

"Mmm...well, that won't be a problem tonight. You're already done with work for the day, so that only leaves us with pleasure. No mixing involved."

In a blink of an eye, he moves in. The distance separating us diminishes as his body cages me in. The back of the chair acts as a bed and his body becomes my blanket. I glance around wide-eyed. How did I get myself in this position? Not that it is a bad position to be in; it's just not one I was expecting tonight.

He presses more of his weight onto me as his words caress my skin. "What do you consider pleasure, Jessica? You spread out, naked, bent over my desk, screaming out my name while I make you come on my fingers. Would that pleasure you?"

Holy shit. I just drenched my panties.

I stare up at him in shock, blabbering like a fool, not only from his words and the images it spurs, but from the bluntness of it all. *Did he really just say that?* This man is seriously messing with my libido and causing my blood to pool in areas it has long deserted. He can easily have any woman he wants, so why me? He must see me as a challenge or a new play thing.

I don't need some rich boy fucking with my head. I've had enough of that to last a lifetime and then some.

My face feels like it's on fire. Licking my parched lips, I shift beneath him, trying to put a semblance of space between us. The move does nothing but rub my boobs against his chest, causing my nipples to harden. Blinking, I try and stay focused.

"Like I said before. I appreciate the offer, all of them, but I must decline," I murmur. "I'm sure you have many women on your speed dial who would be delighted to join you for a meal." I pause, then add. "Or to bend over your desk and scream out your name. Whatever your kink is."

Using his surprise to my advantage, I push around him and go to stand, ready to make a beeline for the door. I need fresh air and time to analyze the frenzied emotions coursing through my body.

Alex follows my motion, snagging my elbow and halting my escape. Turning me to face him, he places his index finger under my chin and lifts my face until my eyes are level with his own. Despite the nervous butterflies battling it out in my stomach, I'm practically panting like some sex-starved lunatic.

I gulp as the warmth of his skin and the smell of his scent surrounds me. My eyes scroll down, hypnotized by his mouth as his tongue slowly darts out and wets his bottom lip. I want that bottom lip. I want to claim it, taste it, and feel it against my skin. Leaning forward he presses his lips against my cheek. I inhale sharply as he moves, planting light kisses down my jawline, across my chin, and back up until he reaches my trembling mouth.

My body is a traitor. It's betraying my mind that is firing off warnings as my body enjoys every scrap of attention it receives. I need to run away. I need to stop him, and yet, I don't.

Alex's hand snakes out, grabbing the back of my neck; he tilts my head back to accept his mouth. I melt into him. The kiss is hungry, carnal, and oh so hot. I moan against his lips as his tongue strokes inside my mouth, scorching everything it touches. I reach my hands up and grasp his broad shoulders for support as my knees threaten to give out on me. I always believed that a girl's knees turning weak over a kiss only happened in the movies. I was wrong about that. So, very wrong.

I shudder as he kisses his way down my throat, nipping and licking the tender flesh in his path. I barely know this man, and yet he works my body like he owns it. His chest is pressed against mine in an instant. Our bodies are meshed tightly together, leaving no wiggle room for escape.

I moan as the evidence of his desire thickens against my stomach. Instinct takes over and I rock against him, grinding myself along his rigid shaft as a dormant desire ignites deep within me.

My nipples pucker through the lace of my bra as his chest brushes against my breasts. I pray he is too busy to notice, but as with most things, I am not that lucky. I groan into my mouth as his hand dips to my breast, cupping it through my shirt and rolling my elongated nipple with his fingers. I whimper as a flood of wetness builds and drips from my aroused sex.

"Damn, baby, you're perfect." His nose grazes against my neck, and I swear I can hear him inhaling.

Is he smelling me?

"You remind me of a ripe peach ready be picked," he growls against my skin.

My nose wrinkles at his odd choice of words.

"Mmm…" are the only sounds I can communicate. His talented hands and warm mouth have me spiraling out of control. In a matter of minutes, he's turned me into a lustful hussy, and for whatever crazy reason, I'm okay with this.

An embarrassing moan leaves my mouth as he continues to grope me, causing my nerve endings to tingle in the most delightful way. Through my haze of lust, I distantly hear my phone sing "Some Nights" by Fun, my customized ringtone for Jane. Hearing that song clears the fog that has taken up residence in my head, and I instantly panic. With a strength I didn't know I had, I forcefully extract my limbs from his.

Steeling my spine, I dig deep and find my voice. "I need to get that. Jane will be concerned if I don't answer. I don't need her calling the cavalry to come find me."

Alex scowls as he studies me. The intensity in his pools of jade bore into me as he dares me to stop what is happening between us. I find myself questioning my own sanity. Alex is dangerous for me. It doesn't take a psychic to figure that one out.

The man oozes sex appeal, and I am sure many women have stood exactly where I am now. The only difference between them and me is that I am not okay with being used for his pleasure. I know for certain this can't go any further. I don't make it a habit to run around kissing strangers, let alone allowing them to feel me up.

With both of my hands pressed against his chest, I take a much-needed breath before using what little strength I have left to push him away. Turning before I have a chance to change my mind, I grab my purse and make my escape.

Moving as if my ass were on fire, I put one foot in front of the other as I try and recall the way back to the elevators. I am almost there when I hear the deep timber of his voice.

His words catch me off guard. "I didn't take you for a coward, Jessica. There is a unique chemistry between us, something I haven't felt in a long time. I know you feel it too," he says, as if challenging me to disagree.

The raw emotion in his voice is almost enough to bring me to my knees. His presence makes it hard to think straight. Panty-dropping kisses and a hot body aside, I refuse to become one of the many notches on his bedpost. I've been used by playboys like him before. I won't do it again.

"It was nice meeting you, Mr. Harlow," I say thickly and reach forward and hammer the elevator call button with clear intent. I let out an audible sigh of relief when the doors open and a car is readily available. Entering it, I press myself into the rear corner and sag against the back wall, feeling as if the weight of the world has been released from my shoulders.

As the doors try to shut, I feel a set of eyes on me. Peering up, I catch Alex watching me. He reminds me of a lion waiting out his time for the perfect chance to pounce, and take down his prey. If he is the lion, I guess that makes me a juicy rabbit.

His voice reaches me as the doors close. "I'll be seeing you soon, Ms. Grayson."

What the hell have I gotten myself into?

Chapter Four

The sun streaming through my bedroom window is an unwelcome invasion. I barely got any sleep last night. I continuously tossed and turned, never able to find a comfortable position. The fact that I am sexually frustrated doesn't help anything. Alex fueled my dreams and my body all night long.

The dream was so real. So much so that I awoke with my panties drenched and my heart hammering in my chest. His mouth was devouring every inch of me, his body positioned snugly amid my legs as his strong hand played with my throbbing sex. His rough voice commanded me, telling me to bend my legs up. Like a puppet tied to a string, I did just that. Using the weight of his body, he keeps them anchored to my chest which leaves my weeping slit bare and open for his perusal. I wasn't embarrassed at all. That should have been my first indication that this was a mere fantasy and not reality.

He kisses his way down my body. I revel in his touch as he nips at my skin, laving the spot with his warm tongue after each love bite. With every exhale, his breath flutters against my heated skin, sending a wave of goose bumps over my sensative flesh. Inching his way down, he positions himself before my core. I peek at him beneath my hooded lids, and the hungry look on his face has my stomach fluttering with anticipation.

When his mouth takes purchase on my pussy, my back bows off the bed, and my fingers thread through his hair. I'm not sure if I am trying to hold him to me or push him away; all I know is that the sensations I am feeling are intense and that mouth of his is what dreams are made of. His tongue licks me from ass to clit, not leaving an inch of flesh unattended to. Like a well-orchestrated dance, his fingers and mouth work in tandem and within minutes my body trembles with a violent orgasm.

Just reliving the dream has me unconsciously squeezing my thighs together. I didn't notice the movement of my hand until it had already trailed down my body and was stroking my wet folds. I can't remember the last time I was this desperate to find a little release.

Shifting beneath the sheets, I open my legs and increase the pressure of my fingers. The pad of my thumb skims over my protruding clit as I tease it with light circles. I groan as the tight bundle of nerves come to life and my need grows. Closing my eyes, I let my imagination take flight and pretend it's Alex's fingers touching me.

Slipping lower, my fingers trace my slit before dipping inside my heat while my other hand travels north and pinches my puckered nipple. It doesn't take long before I am rocking my hips and embracing the build-up in my core. My strokes increase and my breathing becomes ragged as my orgasm bursts forth, hitting me full force. I choke out a cry as I ride wave after wave of the most pleasurable feeling I've felt since... Lord, help me, I can't remember the last time I experienced such bliss.

I'm so screwed. Having Alex affect me this way can't be a good thing.

Dragging my sorry ass out of bed, I head to the shower. The warm water does wonders to clear my mind. After leaving Alex's office last night, I rushed to call Jane back. I kept our discussion to small talk. My mouth opened several times ready to spill all, but each time I ended up changing topics, never able to bring myself to tell her what happened. For whatever reason, I want to keep my encounter with Alex a secret. At least for now.

His last words are still spinning around my battered mind on an endless loop. He said he would be seeing me soon. Was it a simple statement or a warning of sorts? Either way it sounds ominous.

I have no plans to ever see him again. He's dangerous territory. A minefield that would explode in my face, leaving me vulnerable and hurt. I had that happen once before, and like a trouper, I dusted myself off, picked-up the pieces, and put myself back together again. It was the hardest thing I have ever done and not something I take lightly.

Turning off the shower, I grab my towel and quickly dry off as the cold air attacks my warmed skin. Turning towards the mirror I blanch as the fog dissipates and my refection comes into view. My breath catches in my throat as I notice the splotches on my collarbone. No, not splotches, but hickeys. Very dark, very prominent hickeys.

The dirty bastard *marked me.*

I'm panicking. How did I let this happen? I run a light finger over the dark splotches and grimace. They are not pretty, but with a little ingenuity and a lot of luck, I think I can hide them. Being a make-up expert has its perks. Luckily, I've the right tools with me to cover the little buggers up. Alex Harlow should be glad we don't run in the same circles, or he would have a foot shoved up his crotch for pulling this shit.

Throwing on my favorite pair of comfy jeans with a green tank top and sneakers, I scoop up my purse as I head toward the coffee shop around the corner. Normally a cup or two of my trusty generic brand of coffee will do, but today I'm in need of some serious heady java to reguivenate my tired limbs.

Skipping out the door, a gentle breeze sweeps through my hair surprising me. I glance up at the cloudless sky and let the sun warm my skin as I inhale deeply, enjoying the sweet smell of the blossoming magnolia trees tainting the air. The weather today is perfect, which is not something that happens very often in Dallas. I swear Texas has the most bipolar weather. When we are lucky enough to be graced with days like this, where the sun is shining brightly with little to no humidity hanging around, you learn to savor it. I smile brightly. The fresh air is just what the doctor ordered to lift my mood and renews my determination to turn this weekend around. I refuse to let any man, let alone one who thinks he can control me with sex and with a few perfectly placed dimples, pull me down.

****

I was a bum today. Besides painting my toes a funky blue color that reminds me of Cookie Monster's fur and watching movies, I did nothing important. As relaxing as it has all been, I am a bit stir crazy. Grabbing my phone, I call my best friend Jax, my male version of Jane and plead with him to join me for a night of drinks and dancing at Club Twenty-One. It wasn't hard to convince him to go.

For the last few weeks, my dear friend, Jax, has been going to that same club often trying to score a date with a certain female bartender who, for whatever reason, is playing hard to get. Being the opportunist he naturally is, he wasn't going to turn down the opportunity see her again. I don't understand why she keeps turning him down. Jax is a beautiful male specimen, with his sandy-colored hair, light, greenish-grey eyes, a well-toned body, and a heart of gold.

All our close friends, including my bestie Jane, think Jax and I should date. I love Jax more than life itself, but he knows me too well to turn what we have into anything romantic. Maybe if we had met some other way, things could have been different between us. I met Jax through Travis, my previous boyfriend turned fiancé, and my first love.

They were best friends at the time, and when things took a turn for the worse between Travis and me, Jax abandoned his long-standing friendship with Travis and stayed by my side. His loyalty to me has earned him a spot in my heart no one will ever be able to touch. That also means he has seen too much ugliness in my life to turn anything between us into something more. Some lines are never meant to be crossed, and our friendship falls into that category.

With the promise of dancing and alcoholic drinks floating through my mind, I throw on my itty-bitty black, shift dress that stops well above my knees and pair it with my killer blood-red, hooker stilettos. I'm going for the perfect mix of slutty-meets-sophistication.

I spend extra time on my make-up and go for a daring look by emphasizing deep colors around my brown eyes and finishing it all off with a hooker-red lipstick that matches my heels. For once my hair has decided to behave itself as it falls around my shoulders in soft waves instead of the usual frenzied mess that comes from the wonderful Texas humidity. One of these days, I am going to take my mom's advice, and move somewhere that has hair friendly weather. Maybe Colorado or New Mexico.

Glancing at the clock beside my bed, I panic. Jax'll be here in Alex hums quietly. "You are doing it, and he is never late. Taking an extra minute that I don't have, I send a quick text to Jane.

Me: How are you, love? Having fun in the sun?

Jane: Just relaxing. We have had a small change of plans. I'll be back early tomorrow

Me: What? Everything okay?

Jane: Everything is fine. David had to change his plane departure time to Germany due to some problem with work, so we will be coming home earlier than planned. Miss you.

Me: Be careful driving back. I'm going out dancing with Jax tonight. Miss you too.

As I finish up the last part of my text, Jax knocks on the front door. Placing my phone in my purse, I run around the apartment turning off lights and ensuring once more that I turned off the curling iron. Jane is always cursing my horrible habit of forgetting to turn it off. I almost burned down the bathroom one time with the stupid curling iron, and now no one will let me forget it.

A ruggedly handsome Jax greets me when I yank open the door. He is dressed to impress tonight in dark, designer jeans and a charcoal, pullover, short-sleeve shirt that hug his glorious biceps like a second skin.

"You look handsome, sweetie." I lean in as I kiss his cheek. Shooting me a warning look, he runs to the hall mirror to remove the bright-red lip impression on his cheek from my lipstick.

"If that bartender girl turns you down tonight, she needs to get her eyes inspected. I am going to have to beat the girls off you with a stick to get a dance with you tonight," I tease as my eyes rove over his beautiful body.

Leaning down, he dusts a light kiss on my forehead. "You clean up pretty nice yourself, baby doll. And you never have to wait for a dance from me. I'm all yours, anytime you want me."

I duck my head to hide the stupid blush that taints my cheeks. Even when he jokes around, he always says the sweetest things. Every girl needs to hear a nice compliment from a sexy man now and then, even it is from her best friend.

I stand in front of him and do a small twirl. "You don't think the dress is too short, do you? I'm going for sexy and sophisticated tonight, not trashy and easy."

Dramatically rolling his eyes, he laughs. "What's the difference?"

"Sexy and sophisticated, enhances my goods but doesn't let the guy see them. Whereas, trashy and easy, shows off all the goods and makes me a walking billboard for Hookers R Us."

Jax's eyes shoot up in a you-didn't-just-say-that expression that has me laughing out loud. "Hell no. You look sexy. Not easy and far from trashy." Passing by me, he swats my bottom on his way back to the front door. "Let's get going. I'm ready to unwind tonight. It's been a long week at work, and I need a drink."

After locking up the place, he guides me out to his black BMW. I wait impatiently on the curb as he takes his sweet time opening the door before I slide onto the soft, buttery-yellow, leather seats. I love the way the chilled leather feels against my bare skin. Drifting in next to me, he cranks the engine and pulls onto the freeway, heading toward downtown while I make myself useful and play with the radio stations.

Traffic is unusually light for a Saturday night. After singing our lungs out to several Beastie Boys songs, we arrive at the club a little after ten o'clock. With a line wrapping around the side of the building, the place is already packed. Thankfully Jax and the bouncer are gym buddies, and after several manly fists bumps, we are escorted in with little hesitation.

The place is crazy loud as music blares from several carefully placed speakers around the room. While I stand in awe, gushing like a fangirl over the flashing lights and great music, Jax grabs my hand and takes off. He pulls me behind him as he winds his way through the crowd toward one of the last empty tables in the back corner.

I love coming to this club. It is by far one of my favorites due to the upscale decor and classy ambiance. Most clubs I've been to reek of sweat and alcohol, but this one is always clean and hosts an array of up-and-becoming bands.

I carefully climb onto the barstool, holding the bottom of my dress in the process, so as to not flash my goodies. I have a bad feeling I might be fighting with the length of this dress most of the night. As usual, Jax has already caught several stares from the ladies. The fact I'm at his side is not deterring them one bit. Not that I care, but I think they should at least have the decency to see if he is single before giving me the stink eye.

"You okay," Jax asks, observing my scrunched brows.

"Yeah. I'm all right," I respond, just as a perky blonde waitress bounces up, placing two cork coasters in front of us.

"Hi. My name is Lacy. I'll be your waitress. What can I get you two?" she asks casually eyeing Jax as she speaks.

I'm reevaluating my choice of drinking buddy for the night. I never have these problems with I go out with Jane. Of course, she normally has David plastered to her side so that might have something to do with it.

"I'd love a Jack and coke, and Jax," I say pointing a finger at him, "would like a Bud Light in a bottle with no glass." As she turns to walk off, I reach out and tug her arm, gaining her attention. "Lacy, just in case you were wondering. Jax and I are friends. You are free to eye fuck him all you want. I encourage it, in fact," I say, laughing at her blushing face.

Jax gives me a bewildered glance but seems happy with my comment.

"I'll go get your drinks, and thanks for the heads up," she responds, walking away with an extra sashay in her step.

Jax runs a hand down his face as he belts out another harsh laugh. "That was crude, even for you. I can't believe you just said that." Jax whispers, his mouth close my ear so I can hear him over the music.

I shrug. "Sure you can. Don't even try and act irritated with me. She was looking at you like you were a lollipop. Who knows, maybe she was interested in seeing how many licks it would take to find your tootsie roll," I snort. "Plus, she seemed like your type."

Jax gives me a dramatic eye roll that makes me give off another unladylike snort. "You have no clue what my type is," he scoffs. With a hard yank, he pulls my chair closer to his, so we can hear each other without having to yell across the table.

"I most certainly do. You have two main requirements for anyone you deem bed worthy," I answer honestly. "One," I say counting off my fingers, "they have to have a pulse and a vagina that doesn't look like it's been passed around a time or six," I tease. "Second." I hold up another finger. "You always like the perky ones. If they have fake boobs that can salute you and an ass that doesn't sag, they get your attention faster."

Jax's face scrunches up in a horrified look that has me laughing so hard, I'm holding my stomach to stop the pains in my sides. "You make it sound like I'm shallow, baby doll. I know I can be picky, but I'm not that damn bad." He pouts.

He is the only man I've ever met who can pout and still look good doing it. So not fair.

I lean over and give him a chaste kiss on the cheek in a way of an apology. "I'm just playing with you, sweet cheeks. You're my best friend." I bump his shoulder with mine trying to tease a smile out of him. "You know I love you."

He gives me a wink before leaning back and scanning the crowd. We sit in a comfortable silence, both enjoying the music and energetic atmosphere. I have a feeling Jax's week went about as smoothly as mine did. The mood shifts as Lacy prances up to our table with drinks in hand. Her flirting is so transparent, it's sad. She practically slaps him with her boobs as she thrusts them in Jax's face placing our glasses on the table.

Lord, I hope I never become that desperate.

With a saucy wave and a slip of her number, Lacy leaves, shaking everything God gave her and then some. Jax and I share a look before we burst out laughing.

"The girl needs to get a clue and some class. Desperation is not attractive, no matter how great your tits are."

"I agree." I sigh.

The drink feels like silk as it slides down my throat. We spend the first part of the night catching up on work and life in general. The drinks keep coming, and since I never ate a proper dinner earlier, it does not take long before I'm feeling the ramifications of my actions. Between the strong liquor and the energetic atmosphere, my troubles melt away.

Grabbing Jax by the hand, I lead him out onto the dance floor, as Rihanna's song "Umbrella" starts up. We get lost in the music as we bump and grind through several more tracks catching the eyes of those around us. The drinks have made me brave tonight, and my itty-bitty dress is doing its best to keep up with my shaking hips.

Jax might be a pretty boy, but he doesn't dance like one. He moves like a Latin god, with smooth dips and natural transitions that keep me on my toes. His mom was a dance teacher in the town we grew up in. From the stories circulating about, Jax was her star pupil.

Tonight is my night to enjoy myself, and if all goes well, I'll find a tall, dark, and handsome man to take home and dust off the cobwebs between my thighs. With Jax grinding behind me, I pull him closer so he can hear me without having to scream. "I'm parched and need a break so I can cool off."

He nods his understanding and intertwines our hands, pulling me behind him as we make our departure from the dance floor and back to our table. I glance around, looking for Lacy. Noticing her mixing drinks up at the bar, I grab the first waitress who walks by and order us another round.

"So, baby doll, you ready to tell me what's got you so worked up?" Jax's eyes narrow as he watches me.

From previous experience, I know what a patient man he can be. He will wait me out until I finally give in and spill my guts. It's a characteristic I find annoying. Being the stubborn girl I am, I tilt my chin up in defiance and keep my lips sealed. No matter what he throws my way, I won't spill. It perturbs me that he can read me so well. What would I even say; *I met this mystery man who turned out to be my rich and devastatingly beautiful employer. Oh, and, by the way, he wants to make me scream out his name while he fucks me senseless.*

No, thank you. That is not a talk I feel like having.

"I'm good. We came here to have fun, so no doom and gloom tonight. Please," I plead.

He eyes me curiously but drops the subject. Moments later, our new waitress arrives with our drinks. She quickly places each down in front of us and then without another word, takes off like her pants are on fire. I call out and try to grab her attention, wanting to let her she made a mistake, but she is ignoring my advances and keeps going.

I glance down at my drink with raised brows before looking over at Jax's with a frown. She gave me a glass of ice water. Plain, old, boring ice water, while Jax got the beer he requested. Parched, I go ahead and drink the water, but keep my eyes on the lookout for Lacy, and make a grab for her as she passes us.

"Hey Lacy, would you mind getting me another Jack and Coke, please?"

She smiles at Jax, keeping her eyes locked on him as she answers me. "Sure. Let me tend to the table in the corner, and then I will be right back with it."

Jax looks confused, so I explain the other waitresses' drink mistake. I shifted uncomfortably in my seat, feeling excessively hot and sweaty from all the dancing. The crowd of bodies filling the room are turning the place more into a sauna instead of a club. Excusing myself, I head to the ladies' room to freshen up.

Fighting my way through the crowds I breathe a sigh of relief once inside the cold, tiled bathroom. Out of habit, I check my phone to make sure I haven't missed any messages. None for me.

Seeing my reflection in the mirror, I'm appalled at how worn-out I look. Using a damp paper towel, I rinse off all of the caked sweat from my face, then carefully re-apply my lip gloss and some powder on my nose. My wayward hair is another beast of its own. Using a rubber band from my purse I do the only thing possible and throw it up into a ponytail before heading back to our table.

Sliding onto the bar stood, I glance down before me and frown. 'What the fuck?" I glare at Jax as my temper begins to rise. I don't get mad often, but when I do, you better be prepared to get your ass handed to you.

"Are you trying to play a joke on me? If so, I'm not finding it funny, and I wish you would stop," I snap.

His forehead is scrunched in worry. "What's wrong, baby doll?" His voice is honest and full of concern, so I know my anger is misplaced. He doesn't deserve my ire.

I take a deep breath to calm my nerves before I speak. "I ordered a Jack and Coke from Lacy, earlier, and what did I get? Another stupid glass of iced water. What the hell is wrong with the staff here?" I complain loudly.

Searching out Lacy, I find her up at the bar, busy retrieving more drinks. I wait until she is near our table before calling out her name. Glancing up, I watch her face pale, and her movements falter as she makes her way over to us.

"Lacy, where is the drink I ordered? And why the hell do I keep getting served water?" I demand.

"Umm...I'm sorry. We've been ordered to only to serve you water."

Jax and I both stare wide-eyed at each other, astonished at her admission. Besides being flabbergasted, I'm outraged. On several occasions, I've left this bar, stumbling over my own feet, and not once has a waitress or a bartender ever tried cutting me off. I don't understand why now. And why only me and not Jax?

"I would like to have a word with your boss, please," I demand harshly, leaving no room for compromise.

Her eyes dip in concern, but instead of arguing, she nods and agrees to notify him right away. Jax glances at me sympathetically. Lacing our hands together, he gives me a reassuring squeeze.

"Baby doll, why don't we leave and go over to Daven's Place for a few hours and have drinks there? I know it's not your favorite place, but the music isn't too bad. Plus the drinks are cheaper. I'm not sure what's going on here, but you shouldn't have to put up with this bullshit."

I scrunch up my nose in reluctance, but I can't argue that he doesn't have a good point. Just as I am on the verge of agreeing with him, I hear a familiar voice behind me. One that does not make me happy. In fact, I can't remember the last time I have been so pissed off.

"I was told you would like to speak with me, Ms. Grayson."
Oh, hell no!
The fine hairs on the back of my neck prickle with aware-ness. So much for going a whole night without thinking

about *him*. And I was doing so well too. I grind my teeth together in annoyance. I don't want to turn around and look at him, but the magnetic pull he has on me, has me doing just that. The moment I tilt my head up and lock eyes with him, I'm a goner. Pinned in place by his intense stormy green orbs, I can't look away.

"You own this place?" I bite out, an edge of my anger dripping from each word.

"Yes," he answers with ease, his deep voice sounding like a symphony to my ears. "Among other things. Unlike my mother, I prefer to dabble in other talents and industries. Owning a magazine can become monotonous after awhile."

This bit of information intrigues me. I imaged he was one of those old money types who would continue doing whatever the previous family members did before him. Not that I consider that a bad thing, but it shows no creativity on his part. Curious as to what other businesses he might own, I file those questions for a later time, one which does not involve the presence of Alex Harlow.

Jax's eyes are darting between the two of us. I have no doubt he is filled with a million questions by now. Not that I blame him. I would be the same way. I was never hoping to have to talk about Alex with Jax. It looks like that cat is already out of the bag.

Before I have a chance to address the elephant in the room, Alex is already reaching around me, and thrusting his hand out in front of Jax. "I'm Alex Harlow, owner of this establishment, and an intimate friend of Jessica's. Who might you be?"

Jax glares at me, his eyes demanding the answer to the same question running rampant through my head. *Since when did you become intimate with this guy?* I give him the briefest of nods, trying to indicate that Alex is full of shit, and we'll talk about it all later. His eyes calm with acknowledgment.

Jax reciprocates Alex's gesture and shakes his outstretched hand. "I'm Jax Lancaster, a very close friend of Jess's, and her protector from assholes."

I snicker at his comment, loving that he called Alex an asshole. At least I'm not the only one who thinks so. Turning back to Alex, my lips pinch into a hard line as I glare daggers into his chest.

"Why the hell did you tell everyone to serve me water? If I desired water, I would have stayed home, not gotten dressed up in shoes that hate me and a dress that barely covers my ass."

Alex's nostrils flare, the only indication he is not happy with me. "Watch your tone, Jessica. A foul mouth does not suit you," he replies, his voice clipped.

My eyes roll in irritation. "I'm not in the mood for games, big guy. Just answer the question. Why did you interfere in my night and screw with my drink orders? I'm far from trashed. A little tipsy maybe, but I could walk a straight line if required." My voice has risen once again, netting a few odd glances from those around us.

I try and keep my eyes locked on his, but they have a mind of their own as they roll up and down his body, feasting on his dark, good looks. He looks downright edible, dressed in a crisp, white, button-down shirt with sleek, black dress pants that cling to his muscled thighs and perfectly shaped ass.

I try to keep my gawking to a minimum, but judging from his raised brows, I'm failing miserably.

"You've had your fair share of alcohol tonight," he says with a frown. Reaching out he brushes his palm lightly across my cheek. "You refuse to slow down, so I took matters into my own hands and made the decision for you." Leaning over my chair, he pins me with his eyes, daring me to disagree.

I only shrug, not giving away the fact that I'm seconds away from tearing into him. Hurting a client, even one as annoying as Alex, would be bad for business. "You don't get to dictate what or how much I drink," I reply angrily. "You are nothing but an arrogant control freak who needs to learn about boundaries."

His presence has thrown a wrench in my carefree night on the town. Not only are my nerves frayed but my good mood has taken a nose dive. Glancing over my shoulder, I catch Jax's attention. "I think your earlier suggestion was a good one. I need to get out of here and find some real fun."

Jax relaxes back in his chair looking far too pleased with our back and forth banter. Noticing that I'm serious, he jumps out of his chair and is quick on his feet. "Sounds like a plan to me. Let me pay our tab, and I'll be right back. Are you going to be okay here without me?" He asks shooting Alex a warning look.

I smile up at him adoringly. I scored the motherlode when it came to best friends. Between him and Jane, I am the luckiest girl around. I give his shoulder a reassuring squeeze.

"I'll be okay. Mr. Harlow here might act like an ass, but he would never hurt me. I'll wait for you here."

The moment Jax is out of earshot, Alex steps up close to me and places his arms on either side of me, caging me in against the table. My eyes widen as my heart picks up speed. Leaning down, he places his lips against my ear and speaks low so only I can hear. "Jessica, you are trying my patience tonight," he growls low. "That dress of yours is killing me. Every man in here has been eyeing you all night. They can't keep their eyes off you while imagining what it would be like to fuck you. Wondering what that sweet pussy of yours would feel like wrapped around their hard dicks. And to make it all worse, you go and drink too much, shaking your ass all over my dance floor, tempting all of these sick bastards."

His eyes blaze through me as his temper unravels. I stare up at him in shock as my mouth hangs open from his brazen words. Why the hell is he mad at me? I'm the one who has been wronged here, not him. His words piss me off and turn me on at the same time. I refuse to let him get the best of me and damn him for thinking he has any say in what I do. He has no clue the can of whup-ass he just opened.

I lick my bottom lip seductively as I flutter my eyes his way. "First off, my dress covers up all the essentials. It might be short, but it's appropriate for this club. Your club, of all things. Second, maybe I want all these men to look at me. Did you ever consider I might be itching for one of these horny, rowdy men to take me home and fuck me until the sun comes up? Care to make a wager on whose name I will be screaming out tonight?"

I know I'm pushing all of his buttons. The alcohol has given me false courage. Alex does not know me and besides being a client, he has no say in what in my personal life.

Alex scowls at me, his breath is coming in short pants as his chest heaves.

Poking the bear might not have been one of my best ideas.

I glance past him, wishing Jax would hurry the hell up. He's talking to the lady bartender friend he is crushing on, and neither seem in a rush stop anytime soon. Boys and their stupid hormones.

Alex places a finger under my chin and tilts my face, bringing my eyes to meet his and making me lose sight of Jax. Despite the warmth of the room, goose bumps light up my arms.

"First of all, you curse too much. You're not a sailor, so stop trying to talk like one," he orders. "Second, the only person's name you'll be calling out during sex is mine, Ms. Grayson." He slides one hand behind my head to cradle my neck while his other hand possessively grips my waist. The heat from his palm sends a spark through my body that lands straight between my legs.

"I don't know what it is about you, Jessica, but you've consumed my thoughts from the moment we met. I'm an ass, you're right about that, but you still want me. You can try and play off your reaction to me as nothing, but every time I touch your skin, you tremble for me."

The air around us feels thick as I struggle to suck in enough air to respond. I drag my eyes away from his lips, trying to stop remembering the soft way they skimmed over my skin. I hate the emotions he spurs in me; they invoke a weakness in me that reminds me of the girl I used to be. The one who allowed her boyfriend to walk all over her.

I am not that girl anymore!

Squaring back my shoulders, I push down my roaring hormones and give him my best scowl. "You're wrong, Mr. Harlow. Your arrogance is out of control. The tremble you feel from me is not from desire. I don't need you looking out for me. I have Jax for that." I wear my best poker face and pray he buys into my bluff.

His quiet laugh vibrates through his chest into mine. "Good try, Jess. You're a horrible liar," he volleys back. "If you expect me to believe you're not attracted to me, you might want to do a better job hiding the evidence."

I swallow hard as a knot of worry tightens in my belly. "What evidence would that be?"

Placing a hand on my chest, he keeps me close. "If you didn't want me, your heart wouldn't be beating so hard. You would be calm, not riled up or caring what I had to say. Plus," he adds, his voice but a whisper against my ear. "Your nipples wouldn't be hard for me, and I would be spelling your sweet perfume right now instead of your seductive arousal.

I gasp in embarrassment, but he ignores the sound and continues. "You want me the same as I want you. Playing hard to get won't get you anywhere. I'll have you in my bed, underneath me soon enough. It won't be tonight, but when it does happen, you'll be all *mine*, Jessica. I don't share, so if your friend Jax is anything more than the close friend he says he is, you need to send him on his way. Otherwise, I'll get rid of him myself."

Holy mother of all orgasms!

My hands ball into fists by my sides. I have so much I want to say, but I'm afraid if I open my mouth, things will spew out that I might later regret. His arrogance surpasses anything I've ever dealt with. Before I have a chance to retaliate, Jax slides in behind me, placing a comforting hand on my lower back, and steers me away from Alex.

"Ready to go, baby doll?" he asks, glancing impatiently at Alex.

"Of course," I answer. I plaster a fake grin on my face as I lean into Jax's touch.

With Alex still hovering in my personal space, I shove past his chest, causing him to take a step back. I steal glances at Alex as we make our exit, half expecting him to pounce on me as I follow Jax's lead. My legs tremble with nervous energy as I hurry through the crowds.

The cooler night air is refreshing on my over-heated skin. Throwing an arm around my shoulder, Jax pulls me against his side, as we continue toward his car. "You've got to tell me, about him, baby doll. My head is spinning. What the hell just happened in there?"

"I don't even know where to begin. Is there any way I could persuade you to drop it for tonight and let me fill you in later?" It's not that I don't want to tell Jax everything, I know there is no getting around that now. I just don't feel like recapping on the drama right now.

Jax laughs; the sound is infectious. "No way, no how. You are not getting off that easy. Whatever that was in there between you two, it was crazy. I wasn't sure if you two were going to kill each other or rip each other's clothes off and go at it on the table."

I make a huffing noise and punch him in the shoulder. I might be in a dry spell, but I'm not that bad off.

I wait until we are seated back in the safety of his car and speeding down the freeway before I finally cave. Sighing loudly, I give in and tell him about the incident at work, and more importantly, what happened after work.

When I'm finished, he just stares back at me with a goofy smile on his face. "How do you feel about him? Is it merely a physical thing or do you think there could be more between you two?" Leave it to Jax to get right down to the heart of the matter.

The way he asked instantly has me on the defensive. I open my mouth to smart off about how I want nothing to do with the Adonis of a man, but I can't force the words out. Irritated with my unwillingness to lie, I choose my words carefully and settle for something more honest.

"A part of me is intrigued by Alex. I won't disagree that he lucked out in the looks category, but it's more than that. As stupid as it sounds, I think I like that he challenges me. He is complicated and has that whole sexy, brooding thing going for him that mothers warn their little girls away from."

I shrugged when his brows shoot up and look down at the imaginary fuzz on my dress. "It doesn't matter. No matter what I feel or don't feel, the ending is always the same. He is bad news. Nothing can come of it," I add softly, still refusing to meet his gaze.

"Why? Is this because of Travis?"

I huff, angrier than I should be. "Not everything has to do with Travis," I bite back defensively. This is exactly why I didn't want to have this conversation with him. Jane would shoulder past my insolence and move on, but not Jax. Nope, Jax can never let anything go without a fight.

I reach for the radio controls and skip through channels, never landing on one long enough to hear a complete song. "I can't go back to that kind of relationship, Jax. Rich, controlling men like them are all the same. I can't take that type of chance. Travis almost destroyed me, and I refuse to fall back into that destructive pattern."

His hand folds over mine and pulls it into his lap, where he holds it while rubbing soothing strokes over my knuckles with his thumb. An exasperated sigh leaves him as he speaks, clearly ignited by our talk. "Baby girl, money and powerful do not always equal hurt. You can't keep putting all guys into the same category. It's not fair. You're smarter than that. I'm not saying that I agree with Alex's tactics, but in his defense, he does seem pretty damn crazy about you."

"Crazy being the optimum word," I huff, laying my head against the cold glass as I stare out the window. "I know not all guys are like my sadistic ex, but I don't think I'm ready to jump back into that boat yet. There are millions of other ordinary men in the world who could sweep me off my feet."

"Yeah, there are," he agrees. "But will they make you feel the way he does?"

I chew on his words before responding. "God, I hope so."

Chapter Five

Slowly he peels off my shirt, throwing it to the ground as his lips skim over my skin, leaving hot kisses in their wake. Needing to feel the sensation of skin against skin, I reach up and begin working the buttons of his dress shirt. Once open, I slide it over his shoulders, letting it fall and adding it to the growing pile of discarded clothing on the floor.

My hands outline the contours of his chest, marveling at its beauty and muscled form. On a moan, Alex seizes control of my mouth. The kiss is hungry, desperate, and oh so perfect. I hear a faint ringing in the recess of my mind, but ignore it and concentrate on the ache growing in my core.

Wanting more, I reach for his belt. My fingers make quick work of it as he releases my bra clasp with ease. My breasts spill out, aching to be touched. I need him like I need my next breath. To my dismay, the annoying ringing begins once again, sounding louder than before.

Jostled from the most realistic erotic dream I've ever had the pleasure of having, I sleepily pry my eyes open. The ringing continues, as my damn cell phone goes off for the zillionth time. Throwing out my arm, I blindly feel out the top of my side table until my fingers land on it. Through bleary eyes, I stare at the screen in confusion. I don't recognize the number flashing back at me.

Panic grips me. It's two o'clock in the morning, and the only reason someone would be calling me at this hour was if there was a problem or an accident. Concern over the idea of Jane or Jax being hurt has me frantically hitting the accept button.

"Hello?" I rasp, my voice sounds rough with sleep.

"Are you alone?" A commanding voice barks out.

"Huh?" I pull the phone away from my ear and stare at the screen again, wishing it would shed some light on whom I'm speaking with. Nope. The number is foreign to me. "Who is this?" I inquire my confusion boarding on annoyance.

"Ouch," the voice rumbles. "If you've already forgotten me, then I'm losing my touch. I'll work on leaving a stronger impression with you next time." His husky voice strikes a chord that resonates through my body.

I suck in a harsh breath. "Alex?" I ask in disbelief. "I never gave you my phone number. Has anyone ever told you that stalking is creepy, not to mention illegal?"

He chuckles, the sound making my stomach flip. "You never answered my question, Ms. Grayson. Did you go home alone tonight or is someone with you?"

As much as I would love to yank his chain and see how he would react by telling him I was worn out from a satisfying night of sex, I'm too tired to play those games. Instead, my mind wanders back to my sexy dream he interrupted. With a sigh, I give him the answer he wants to hear.

"I'm alone. I wasn't lying earlier when I said Jax is only a friend. Not all men are like you. There are a few still left in the world who can connect with the opposite sex and not want to fuck them, Mr. Harlow," I hiss through the phone.

"You have a filthy mouth," he says with disdain.

I roll my eyes. I'm used to hearing my mom say the same thing. If her warnings couldn't stop me from cursing, his definitely won't.

"Contrary to any gossip you might've heard or read in the press, I don't go around fucking everyone I meet."

I laugh under my breath, not trusting his evaluation of himself. "I answered your question. Now it's your turn. How did you get my number?"

"It was on the business file your partner filled out for the magazine," he says smoothly, as though using my company file for personal reasons is an everyday occurrence. It might be. I can't help but wonder how many other women he has propositioned at work. A ping of jealousy runs through me. I don't want to be one of many. I want to be unique and different from all the others.

I shake off that prospect, not liking the route it's taking. "That was for work purposes only," I accuse on a yawn. "You're screwing with my sleep, Mr. Harlow. Now that you know I'm not busy shagging someone, can I go back to sleep, or was there something else you needed?"

I grin, remembering my naughty dream. He would be beside himself if he knew I was dreaming about having sex with him.

"I was just checking on my investment, Jess. Making sure you understood my earlier warning. I meant what I said before. I'm a selfish bastard. I won't tolerate sharing you with anyone. Sweet dreams, baby girl. I'll be seeing you soon."

The line goes dead before I can respond or ask how the hell I became *his* when we've never dated. And who the hell calls another person an investment? That shit is creepy. Holding my pillow to my face, I scream as loud as I can into it. I have never met a more infuriating man.

****

I wake to voices drifting from the living room. A smile creeps across my face, realizing Jane is finally home. I stretch out lazily, my arms and legs extending in opposite directions as my muscles flex and relax. Throwing my legs to the floor, I climb out of bed and head straight for the shower. The warm water helps bring me back to life, but with it come memories of my erotic dream, staring the one and only, Alex the asshole. Remembering the way he kissed and licked my skin has my body humming again.

I have to find a way to flush him from my system.

I generally date guys who tend to be more on the submissive side of the scale. The type who allow me to keep the upper hand and happily go along with whatever I choose. It's not that I am a control freak or anything, I just prefer to date men who are the complete opposite of my first love, Travis.

Alex does not fall into that category, which scares and excites me at the same time. I would be lucky to retain a sliver of control with him. He's a master at keeping me off kilter.

I don't understand him. No rational person becomes possessive of another after a few stolen kisses. We haven't even made it to third base yet, and he is already trying to dictate my actions.

Examining my pruned fingers, I hurry to finish my shower before the hot water fizzles out on me. I'm anxious to see Jane again. We have so much to catch up on, and I am dying to hear about her weekend away with dipshit David.

Stepping out of the shower, I pull my cozy, chenille robe around myself to ward of the cooling air and then twist a towel around my hair before heading down the hall. My grin only grows wider as I spot Jane in the kitchen, pouring herself a cup of coffee.

"Good morning, sunshine," she says smiling back at me. "I see you managed not to burn down the apartment while I was gone." Her eyes light up with mirth as she teases me.

I shake my head as I hold back a laugh. "You're never going to let me live the curling iron incident down, are you? One mistake and I'm scorned for life. So not fair." I eye her cup of coffee with want.

She follows my eyes and gives me an impish grin. "Care for a cup?"

I nod, inhaling the heavenly scent of fresh-ground coffee beans still dancing in the air. "Yes, please." I plop down on a bar stool.

She goes over to the cabinet and retrieves my favorite coffee cup from the top shelf.

"So, how was it? Was the lake house everything you hoped it would be?"

"The weather was beautiful. I enjoyed having David all to myself, but as always, he couldn't leave work alone for more than a few hours before going through paperwork withdrawal. I swam in the lake and laid out while he caught up on emails." She fidgets with a stray strand of hair as a pout pulls at her lips. I hate seeing Jane so deflated. Knowing David caused it makes me want to squash him like the bug he is.

"It sucked. I could have been there alone for as much time as he spent with me. It wasn't the romantic weekend I had hoped for," she adds while moving around the kitchen fixing my coffee just the way I like it. Adding the right amount of milk and sugar, she gives it a stir then passes it over.

I can tell she's in a funk, and I don't like it. One of the best things about Jane is the spark of light she always has in her eyes. Right now her spark seems to be lost. In my eyes, David is a soul sucking leech, but to keep our friendship out of rocky terrain, I've always kept my feelings about him under lock and key. If David is half the douche I think he is, it won't be much longer before he slips up, and Jane sees him for who he is. I just hope she doesn't get too hurt in the process.

Sipping my coffee, I offer to be the friend she needs right now, and just be there for her and let her vent while she works through her feelings. We spend most of the day doing just that while vegging out and watching a few action flicks.

Curled up on the sofa, I continue to work the silver polish over my nails while *Men in Black* plays on the television. When I least expect it, Jane ambushes me. "You ready to tell me about your weekend? A little birdy told me it was one for the records."

Turning toward her, I keep my face blank as I feign ignorance. "I don't know what you mean. Nothing much happened. Pretty boring actually." Her eyes narrow at me, and it takes everything in me not to squirm. Jane missed her calling as a lawyer, her interrogation tactics are that good.

"I got a text from Jax today. He was asking me how you were doing. When I pushed to find out why he would be concerned about you, his stupid butt tried and failed to play it off as nothing. You two are the worst liars around." She gives me the evil eye. "Spill it, Jess. What are you trying to hide from me?" She raises her brows at me, letting me know this conversation is not going away. It's one of those classic mom moves. Not my mom, of course, but one of those caring moms you would see on TV. My mom never cared enough to know if I was holding something back or not.

Sitting my bottle of polish down on the coffee table, I sink further into the sofa cushions, wishing they would swallow me up and hide me from her inquisitive questions. *Where to even begin?*

With a loud sigh, I tell her everything. Beginning with the job shoot, my meeting in Alex's office, his intrusion on my night out clubbing with Jax and end it with his call last night. When I'm done talking, she is staring back at me with a stupid ass grin smeared across her face.

"So," she begins, her voice highlighted with humor. "You have *the Alex Harlow* wanting to sweep you off your feet and instead of pissing on his leg and claiming him, you're running away from him? What the hell is wrong with you?" She throws her hands up in mock terror before throwing a pillow at my head.

"No," I object loudly, catching said pillow and tucking it behind me. "He has no plans to sweep me off my feet. He wants to fuck and own me. Last time I checked, those two things are in no way similar."

I ignore her roar of laughter as I reach for my soda, wishing it was mixed with something stronger. A little liquid courage is always needed for such conversations. "Stop laughing. I enjoy my quiet life with little to no drama." I throw my head back on the couch with a huff. "What am I going to do, Jane?" I ask, worry coating my words. "The man is hard to say no to. He's gorgeous, annoying, and for some stupid reason, I want to like him.

She gives me a bewildered look that makes me want to scream with frustration. "I don't see the problem."

"He's a playboy. I'm not delusional about how men like him work. He'll have sex with me, deliver earth-shattering orgasms, and then leave me. I don't want to feel used again," I admit, my cheeks blushing with the admission.

Sliding across the cushion to my side of the sofa, Jane takes my hand and entwines it with hers. "Jessica, you've got to stop thinking all men will use you the way Travis did. He was one horribly rotten apple surrounded by a bunch of good ones. You can't judge everyone by his standard."

I can feel the atmosphere shifting toward darker territory, and I don't like it. My friends shouldn't always be left to deal with my issues. Refusing to let my past mistakes ruin our day, I thank her for caring and quickly change the subject.

"Want to go out to eat tonight? My treat," I add hoping it will help to entice her to agree.

"I'm not a cheap date," she answers with a laugh. "Will dessert be included?"

I nod, glad she takes the bait and is agreeing to drop the subject of my non-sex life. Jane and I have this ritual we always do. Every time we go out to eat, I order a sinful, calorie and fat enriched dessert, and each time she promises to help me eat it. Once it's delivered to the table, she takes a bit or two, and then I'm left eating the rest all by myself. I blame her for the extra pounds that keep magically appearing on my hips. Sure, I could take a few bites myself and leave the rest, but I always feel bad wasting something so heavenly. Uneaten dessert should be a crime.

"Always is," I answer, playfully slapping at her leg. "Let's get dressed. Last one ready has to drive," I call out, already up and dashing down the hallway to my room.

Jane calls me a cheater while letting loose a string of curses after stubbing her big toe on the door frame of her bathroom. I inwardly groan, knowing I'll be blamed for her klutz move. Jane is never at fault for her two left feet. You can be halfway across town or the world for that matter, and my sweet Jane will always find a way to blame you for one of her numerous self-induced accidents.

She's a big baby.

Clothed—*check*, teeth brushed—*check*, hair styled in a loose ponytail—*check,* and sandals buckled. *All checked.* All I need is to finish my make-up, and I will beat Jane for the first time. Finally, I can almost taste the sweet victory.

We've been racing against each since our college years, and I always lose. That ends tonight. I'm determined to win. Pulling out my pink bag from underneath the sink, I lay out the basics—powder, blush, lip gloss, and black mascara—and get to work.

Slathering on my final layer of mascara, I shove everything back under the sink and run back to my bedroom in search of my purse. Not two steps through the door and my phone begins to sing "Crazy" by Aerosmith, a ringtone I set for Alex after his late-night phone call. I glare at the phone, contemplating whether or not I should answer it.

Eeny, meenie, minie—nope, not answering it!

Until I have time to figure out how I want to handle the man, I need to stay away from him. No contact means no temptation, and that is all he is to me right now. A huge freaking temptation to sin. Sighing heavily, I hit the reject button and toss my phone into the depths of my purse.

I sprint back into the living room seconds before Jane comes barreling in. I dance around the room like a lunatic, delighting in my win while making a point to rub it in her face.

"I let you win. You know that, right?" she says, shaking a finger at me as she retrieves her car keys.

I shake my head in denial. "You wish. You're such a sore loser," I joke as I follow her out to the car. My phone begins singing "Crazy" again. Digging it out of my bag, I quickly swipe at the screen and hit the reject button. Jane glances my way, her brows arched in question.

"What do you want to eat?" I ask, not giving her a chance to ask about the phone call. To my delight, she leaves the taboo subject alone, and for once my phone stays silent.

"I am not dressed for anything too fancy. How about Napoli's Italian?"

I shrug. "That works for me. They have good wine, and I'm ready for a glass or four."

Napoli's Italian does not serve the most authentic Italian food, but it's edible and it works in a pinch. Only a few minutes from our apartment, we eat here far more than we should. Upon arriving, we're greeted by a non-enthusiastic hostess who makes it clear by her gum smacking and total lack of eye contact that she would rather be any other place than here seating us.

Following her to a booth near the far side of the room, I slide into my seat just as my phone loudly beeps indicating that I have a new text message. Jane studies me over the menu, her eyes seeing more than they should.

"Someone is persistent tonight. Do I have to guess who it is or are you going to be a good friend and tell me?"

I already know who it is, and yet my eyes still gravitate down to the phone in my hand. Seeing *Master of the Universe* light up on my screen sends me into a fit of giggles.

Giving him that nickname might have been a stretch, but I can't deny it fits his personality. He should never have told me to call him that in his office. What a joke.

I contemplate what to say. A small part of me itches to lie and say its Jax calling, but I hate keeping things from Jane. Lies never end well for anyone involved. Lord knows I would give her hell if I ever found she did the same to me.

I clear my throat. "It's Alex Harlow," I say nonchalantly, acting as though it is not a big deal despite the panic creeping into my chest.

Jane's lips twitch, as she locks eyes with me. "So, would I be correct in saying he's the one who keeps calling? The one with the "Crazy" song ringtone?"

Her scrutiny is too much, and I quickly swing my gaze around the room, latching onto anything but her all-knowing gaze. I nod a small yes. "The song seemed...fitting."

Jane chuckles softly, and I can't help but join in. The heavy weight between us evaporates as our waiter arrives. Already knowing the menu by heart, we order two glasses of the house white wine and fried cheese appetizers.

"What does the text say?"

I let out a long sigh as I pull my phone from my bag. Swiping my thumb across the screen, it lights up illuminating his message. I read the name silently to myself before breaking down letting Jane know what is says.

Alex: Stop ignoring my calls. My good will toward you is deteriorating fast. Answer me, Ms. Grayson before you force me to do something you will regret.

"Wow. You were right. He's intense. What has his underwear in a bind?"

I shrug. "I think it is my bubbly personality and charm that sets him off. I don't think he's used to having to work to get a girl's attention."

She hums and nods thoughtfully. "So, are you going to answer him?" Her question sounds far more cheerful than it should. I can tell Jane is enjoying my newfound drama. I'm not sure how I feel about it yet, but I am leaning toward being intrigued by it all.

I bite my bottom lip as I contemplate what to do. The smart thing would be to ignore him, hope he takes a hint, and gets bored with the chase. Unless it is the chase which keeps him coming back, then I'm screwed.

I've never been good at making a decision under pressure and now is no different. I study my phone as though it will magically give me the right answer. I should invest in one of those silly black eight balls that you shake to get a response to a question you ask. That would be awesome right now. Before I have the chance to do anything, my phone beeps with another incoming text.

Alex: Last chance Ms. Grayson. By the way, I love you in blue.

My eyes immediately trace the blue halter top I threw on before we left the house. I can't breathe. I turn in my seat, frantically searching the restaurant to see where he's hiding. How else would he know what I'm wearing? There are only a few patrons sitting in the restaurant. Unless he has aged thirty years overnight or became a woman, none of them are Alex. Napoli's is not a place I would expect him to grace with his presence. When I think of Alex, I imagine elegance and class, not casual and dumpy.

Sensing my near panic, Jane jumps to attention. "You've gone pale on me. What gives?"

Balls to the wall. The asshat is managing to ruin another night out with a friend. With reluctance, I hand over my phone and let her read the message. Her response matches my own, minus the mini heart attack I swear I'm having. My stomach churns as dry wine floods my taste buds. My mouth is so parched, I down half my glass in one gulp.

Glancing around our room, she slides my phone back to me. "Girl, you've got to respond. Take control and stop being a chicken. Ask him where his fine ass is hiding. You can invite him over if you want. I won't mind," she adds with a wink.

I met her gaze and flinched. "I'm not a chicken," I bite back defensively. I glare at the buttons on my phone, contemplating a smart retort that will put him in his place. When one doesn't come, I give up and settle on the most obvious.

Me: Stalking me now? Behind what potted plant are you hiding? What do you want, Mr. Harlow?

My phone beeps back instantaneously.

Alex: Glad you came to your senses. I don't hide. Come outside. I need to speak with you. Come alone.

Me: Why would I want to do that? And how did you know I was here? I already told you once stalking is a crime.

Alex: No stalking needed. Come outside, and I will answer your questions. You've got ten minutes before I come and retrieve you myself. Tick, Tock.

What the hell?

I can't win. If I don't go outside, he might barge in here and cause a scene, and if I go outside, he gets his way. I tap my fingers on the table while contemplating my options. I check my watch, seeing that I'm down to three minutes before the choice is out of my control.

Throwing my napkin on the table, I half rise from my chair with fists clenched, ready to go into battle. I give Jane an apologetic look.

"Would you mind ordering for me? He's right outside, and I need to nip this in the bud before it gets any worse."

Jane smiles. "Of course I will, but I can't promise there will be any cheese sticks when you return. Do you want your usual? Spaghetti and meatballs with extra sauce?"

I laugh and roll my eyes. "The cheese sticks are all yours, and yes to the spaghetti. Don't let them get away with forgetting the extra sauce. I hate when they do that."

Marching out of the restaurant, I give myself a quick little pep talk along the way. You can do this Jess. He is just another rich jerk who thinks he makes all the rules. Stay strong. Don't back down, and make him want to run for the hills.

Pushing through the double doors, I'm greeted by a gorgeous, black, Mercedes stretch limo. My eyes take it all in along with the intimidatingly large, bald, bouncer type of man, standing guard outside the back door. He is huge. I mean, the man could easily pass for a pro wrestler. His intense and daunting appearance does nothing to calm my nerves. My insides twist into knots as my feet continue toward the car. The bouncer man nods to me as he opens the back door, but refuses to meet my eyes. That can't be a good sign.

I glance into the car but don't see Alex right away. I'm suddenly regretting my decision to come out here. This was a horrible idea. *Why the hell didn't Jane stop me or try to knock some sense into me?* Before I have a chance to turn away and run, the driver places a hand on my back and gives me a slight push. I'm sent sprawling into the car with my ass hanging off the seat in a most undignified way. With a snicker from the brute, the door slams shut.

As my eyes adjust to the darkness around me, I finally see Alex seated on the bench seat across from me. Dressed in a dark-gray suit, he looks like he just came from work. Dragging myself onto the seat, I mutter a curse under my breath as I notice Alex's demeanor. His clenched jaw and furious green eyes don't bode well for how this conversation will turn out.

Fuck. Nothing like being trapped in a small space with an illogical, insanely gorgeous, and pissed off man. Lucky me.

Alex watches me like a hawk. His gaze is calculated and guarded despite that familiar magnetic pull that grows between us whenever we're near each other. I swallow hard and remember my little mental pep talk. No matter what happens, I need to stay strong and not back down.

"Well, you called me out here, so don't waste my time. What was so important you had to trample on another one of my nights out?" He doesn't answer right away, and my anger grows with each passing minute. The ass never has the patience to wait for me. He snaps, and I jump, but when the tables are turned, he always takes his time. Fuck that.

After what feels like forever, he finally speaks. "Why are you ignoring my calls, Jessica?" His tone is bored, but the ticking in his jaw gives away his simmering anger.

I shrug, refusing to apologize for my actions. "I've been busy, plus I didn't have anything to say to you."

The look he returns is just short of hostile. Ignoring it, I continue. "We're not an item, and even if we were, I'm not okay with you thinking I should be at your beck and call, Mr. Harlow. I have a job and friends, and those two things come first for me."

His lips press into a thin line that matches my own. With his elbows balanced on his knees, he steeples his fingers together and rests his chin on them. He is so quiet it worries me. I can see his mind is working again, which never ends in my favor.

When he speaks again, his voice startles me. "You're right, Jessica, we're not officially an item. I think it's time we rectified that."

I panic. "Rectify that? No, no, no. That is not what we need to do."

Reaching across the expanse of the back seat, he yanks me toward him, causing our bodies to crash together. His wide shoulders and muscular arms engulf me, breaking my fall and holds me hostage against his warm body while he kisses me hard. His tongue doesn't wait for an invitation as it dips into my mouth, thrashing wildly with mine, and branding everything it touches. Lifting me slightly, he pulls my legs over his so that I'm straddling him. My achy core unceremoniously lines up against his hard cock, and I whimper softly in pleasure.

I bury my face in his neck as his mouth moves, licking and nipping at any exposed expanse of skin it comes within contact of.

Get a grip, Jess. You need to stop this.

Pulling away, I place a hand on his chest and between harsh breaths, ask the question that has been eating at me. "Why do you want me? You don't know me, and yet you keep coming at me like a dog starved for a bone. Why?"

His eyes pierce me with a hunger I feel down to the tips of my toes. Rubbing at the stubble decorating his chin, he gives me a shy smile. "Ever since you fell in my arms, I can't get you out of my head. I thought it was all about sex at first, but then you went and told me off in my office and as twisted as it sounds, that defiance sealed the deal for me." He pinches a piece of my hair between his fingers and rolls it while he speaks. "I don't make a habit of chasing women, but for you, I will gladly continue until you give me a chance."

I wet my lips as I shift my weight. "That makes absolutely no sense."

"Maybe not, but it's how I feel, and no other woman has ever made me feel as alive as I do when I'm around you." Fisting a hand in my hair, he holds his forehead against mine. His breath tickles my skin as he speaks. "Give me a chance."

My heart explodes inside my chest at his declaration, and before I can talk myself out of it, I reach up and begin fumbling with the knot in his tie. I pull it loose and drop it beside me as I work on his shirt buttons. I'm a woman on a mission, and when a few buttons give me trouble, I yank on them in frustration, causing them to snap and go flying around the back of the limo.

I want to see his body, feel the contours flex under my fingers. He helps me shed his shirt as I undo his buckle and pants. Frantically we work together as one unit until we are both stripped down to our underwear. My breath catches sharply as our eyes connect and hold. The only sound in the car is our hard breathing as we silently dare the other to make the next move.

What the hell am I doing? Do I agree to this, whatever it is, or do I run the hell away, and vow never to look back?

I want this. I want him. What sane, heterosexual female wouldn't? He's gorgeous, powerful, has the world at his feet, and for whatever reason, he wants me. I want his body in every way possible, but I don't want to get attached. Hot sex, I can handle, but I don't know if I'll be able to keep myself detached emotionally. An emotional relationship is not an option. Not for me at least. I have to keep my heart locked away. It's the only way to protect it along with my sanity.

I lick my lips as my eyes skim up and down his delicious body. With his tanned skin, slim hips and toned muscles, he is a walking orgasm waiting to happen.

"What do you want, baby?" His eyes punch holes into me. When he looks at me like he is doing now, I swear he can see through all the thick layers I use to shield myself down to the real me. It's unnerving and exciting at the same time.

"I'm not sure I can do this," I answer honestly.

Leaning forward, he kisses the tip of my nose. On a sigh, I rest my forehead on his as I try to make sense of my jumbled emotions. So much has happened in such a small amount of time, and I'm not sure what to make of it all.

Wrapping his arms around my waist, I moan as his bare skin touches mine. Shifting our weight, he grinds his hard erection against my damp panties. My hands lift and tangle in his hair as my body moves against him, urging him on and loving the feel of him beneath me.

"Stop overthinking it, Jessica," he growls, nipping my ear. "I want you. All of you. Not just your body and not for only one night. Turn off that overactive brain of yours and let yourself feel."

"I don't know how to do that."

"I'll teach you. I need you to trust me and stop fighting this connection we have," he breathes against my lips.

I've lost all sense of what is right or wrong. I'm normally the practical one in my group of friends. They all look to me for answers when they need help, and yet here I sit, confused, horny, and unable to figure out what to do. Whenever Alex is close, my brain malfunctions and goes on the fritz.

I run my fingers over his shoulders as I find the right words to express the notions tugging at me. "You can have my body, but I can't promise you anything else." I sigh in agitation at how unsure my voice sounds. "Just sex. Mind blowing, unattached, monogamous sex."

He pulls my fingers away from his chest, popping them into his mouth and sucking on them in a way that makes my stomach flip in delight. "Okay," he growls. "I'll agree to your terms. At least for now," he says with a wicked grin. The determined gleam in his eyes has me second guessing my ability to play in his league.

He drops my hands and traces an imaginary line across my neck. "Why did you cover up my mark?" His calm voice defies the storm brewing within him. As wrong as it sounds, the fierceness in it excites me.

I blink rapidly and push through the fog of lust I'm lost in. It takes me a moment to realize what he's speaking about. When I finally catch on, I can't stop the smile that overtakes me. I forgot all about the hickey he gave me earlier in the week. Pulling back I give him my best you-are-an-asshole look.

"Just sex, Mr. Harlow. You don't get to mark me as yours. I'm not here for your money, your connections or even your mind, however, wonderful it might be. I just want you, Mr. Strong Arms." I grind my center down on him, letting him feel the heat and need seeping through my pussy. He groans low, the sound vibrating through his chest and into my own. I shudder and repeat the motion.

"Why did you call me Mr. Strong Arms?"

I laugh and curse my stupid slip. I never meant to call him that to his face, but whatever. What's done is done. "Sorry, it's was a nickname I gave you. From when you caught me before I fell on my ass at the photo shoot. "

He chuckles with me, apparently recalling that moment as well. "You know, my love, it is said that a nickname is a term of endearment. I like that you gave me one."

"Maybe it is," I agree with a shrug. "Although, I like to use them to keep my many men separated. A nickname keeps me from calling out the wrong name when I come." I say with a flirty laugh.

He slides his nose along the shell of my ear, as his hands grip my hips, crushing my body against his. My laughter ceases as my breathing picks up, my heart pounding a loud beat against my ribs. Staring into his dark eyes, a delicious shiver runs down my body.

Alex stares at me, contemplating his response. "I know you're joking, so I will let that little comment slide. You should never push me, love. I told you before. I don't share, and I have no qualms running down anyone who gets in the way of something I want." I swallow hard; I have no words. I'm floored by his statement.

"You'll be going home with me tonight, Jessica. I plan on spending the whole night finishing what we started in my office. There will be no more argument about what is and what's not mine, after tonight."

My eyes widen. *Oh...really?*

My lips touch his in a feather-light kiss. I pull away before he has a chance to deepen it. "Ask me nicely, Mr. Harlow," I whisper against his lips.

He smiles, the sight of it is making my body light up like the Fourth of July. "Jessica, would you please accompany me home tonight so I can fuck you endlessly?" he asks, rubbing his fingers seductively against my heavy breasts.

Who could say no to that?

"Yes...yes, I will."

Chapter Six

As he tucks me against him, the realization that we're still at the restaurant seeps through my lust-filled mind, and I panic. Holy hell, I am hands down the worst friend.

I tug on Alex's arm as my anxiety builds. "I left Jane inside. I can't just leave her here. I've got to go back in and explain everything to her and at least pay for my portion of the bill," I say scrambling to find my clothes thrown around the back seat.

"Stop," Alex says, grabbing my hands and halting the small progress I've made. "My driver, Carson, will handle it. You are not walking out on me again," he says soundly. Reaching around my shoulder, he pushes a button on a built-in panel behind the seat.

I watch him cautiously as a man's voice comes through the car's speakers, "Yes, Mr. Harlow?"

"Carson, please go inside the restaurant and let Ms. Grayson's friend, Jane, know she will be accompanying me home tonight. Pay their bill, and have Ms. Grayson's dinner boxed up to go."

"What?" I stammer. "No. I need to go inside. That is beyond rude. I don't blow off my friends this way." I try once again to get dressed, but Alex tightens his grip on me, making it impossible to move.

"You are more than welcome to call her and make your peace, but there is no way in hell I am letting you out of this limo," he says flatly. "You, my love, have a horrible history of bolting."

Control freak!

My exaggerated eye roll and the go-to-hell look I throw his way do not go unnoticed. I can tell he wants to say something, but for once, he keeps his beautiful lips shut.

"Fine," I exhale in defeat. "Can you please release my hands so I may text Jane and throw myself on her mercy?"

He takes a moment to think about it before releasing me. I can feel his eyes focused heavily on me, as though I might dash out the door, and run away half naked at any moment.

That would be interesting. It might be worth the embarrassment just to see him blow his lid.

Carson returns shortly with my meal in hand. I can't see him through the black car partition, but his raspy voice comes over the speaker, letting us know everything has been taken care of. Alex thanks him and we are off. I quickly text Jane.

Me: Please forgive me. I am sorry and realize what a horrible friend I am.

Jane: You are forgiven. I called Jax. He was bored and is on his way here.

Me: I will make it up to you. Not that it's an excuse, but Alex is being a bit controlling and contrite tonight.

Jane: Never believed I would see the day, but you've finally met your match.

Me: We'll see about that. I will be home tomorrow morning, early enough to head into work with you.

Jane: Okay, sounds good. Be careful. Call me if you need anything.

I throw my phone back in my purse on a sigh. Reaching across the seat, I collect my shirt, bra, and skirt with the intention of redressing before we reach Alex's home. I wonder what type of home he has. Will it be a lavish condo or an obscenely huge mansion?

I manage to get my bra refastened, but the rest of my clothes are ripped from my hands, and thrown across the seat. Warm hands hook around my waist, and I'm yanked back onto his lap. My protest goes unanswered as his lips devour mine. The kiss is possessive and hungry in a manner that takes my breath away and has me begging for more.

I ache to touch him all over as I place light kisses on his face, throat, and lips. I run my hands through his hair and use it as an anchor to pull him closer to me. The man reeks of sex and that familiar cinnamon and vanilla scent I've become familiar with.

With one hand still holding my waist, his other hand trails down my neck to my chest. His fingers encircle my breast, squeezing it roughly through my bra and making me gasp. My body is on fire and completely aroused. My silky panties are ruined and soaked as warm liquid seeps from my core.

I push down, grinding my soaked center against his cock, and my pussy quivers with anticipation. Moaning my name, Alex rasps his teeth against my shoulder before biting down, sinking his teeth in just enough to mark me once again. Bypassing the fact, he ignored my request not to leave any evidence on my skin, I relish that I can drive him as crazy as he does me.

"You are so beautiful, Jessica. My beautiful Jessica," he murmurs. His voice is rough with need.

"I want you, Alex," I whisper against his lips. His eyes glisten as they travel over me, memorizing every inch of my body.

"Not here, baby. My first time in you isn't going to be in the back of a car," he whispers. My insides quiver with excitement. Slipping a hand down between our bodies, the heel of his hand lands firmly on my pussy as he cups it tenderly. I bite back a needy moan as his finger slides through my slick folds. His lids lower, and the open desire on his face is almost enough to make me lose it.

"Damn, baby, you're drenched. Lean back and let me take care of you."

Gripping my waist, he lifts me off his lap and lays me down on the seat beside him. I let out a sigh as the cool leather presses into my heated skin, sending goose bumps across my exposed flesh. My eyes stay trained on him, watching his every move with anticipation.

His arrogant gaze travels down my body and despite my best intentions, I can't help but want him. Pulling my face to his, he softly kisses my lips while his fingers work at peeling back the cups of my black lace bra.

I arch my back and thrust my chest forward as my breasts spill out, begging for his touch. As if reading my mind, his hand palms my breasts, squeezing and pinching my taut nipples as my arousal rises. My flesh throbs with the need to feel him against me. I try and pull him closer to me, but am stilled as his free hand grabs my wrists and pulls them above my head, immobilizing my movements. My eyes widen in surprise.

"You look so sexy like this," he says with complete admiration. "I can't wait to see you tied to my bed, my cock thrust deep inside you while you beg for release. If you're a good girl, I might even let you."

My voice fails me as the lump in my throat robs me of any response. My breathing has turned shallow, and my heart is pounding out a rhythm so fast and loud, I'm surprised he can't hear it.

His mouth grazes my skin as his tongue darts out, licking the tip of my taut nipple. Taking it into his hot mouth, he rolls it around with his tongue while gazing up at me. I try and keep my eyes locked on his, but with the way he's touching me, loving me, it's too much, and I eventually close them and just feel, enjoying it all.

Nipping my nipple lightly with his teeth, Alex moves to my other breast and gives it the same attention. I moan as the heat in my belly expands to every fiber of my being. The feelings he is invoking in me are exquisite and raw.

"Your mouth is very talented," I all but purr.

He chuckles. "Wait till you see what I can do with my cock."

Oh...please, show me. Now!

My breathing goes into overdrive as he trails kisses down my stomach, licking in and around my belly button before stopping just above my throbbing clit. He pauses and looks up at me through his thick lashes. "You smell heavenly, baby. I've been dying to taste you. I bet you're sweet and juicy like a peach."

"Please," I beg. "Do it." I barely recognize my voice. It sounds raspy and hoarse, so, unlike my usual self.

"Do what, baby?" He draws out, his warm breath teasing the sparse hair on my pubic mound.

I shoot him a murderous glare, which makes him laugh. He plants wet kisses all over my inner thighs and legs but restrains himself from ever touching my clit or weeping slit. I shudder and squirm all over the seat trying to steer him closer to where I need his mouth the most, but he keeps moving everywhere, but there.

I don't think I've ever been this frustrated or horny before. It's pure torture. I don't know if a person could die from sexual frustration, but if they could, I would be pushing up daisies about now. I let out a frustrated growl that impresses even me.

Propping up on one arm Alex stops and looks me straight in the eyes. "Tell me what you want, Jessica," he commands. "I can play this game all night. Just a few simple words and all this nonsense can be over. Use that pretty mouth of yours to speak, and then I will gladly use my tongue and make you come."

Biting my bottom lip to stifle an aggravated scream, I weigh my options, which are very few. With my head held high, I throw caution to the wind and give in. Humiliation be damned, I need his mouth on me like no other. "Lick me. Please stop teasing me and lick my pussy, my clit, and everywhere in between," I plead.

I want to crawl into the seats and hide the blush staining my cheeks, but I have nowhere to go. This is all a first for me. I have never had to verbalize what I want from a man before. The few men I have been with have always taken what they want. I lay there while they did their thing and hung on and enjoyed the ride. Having to articulate my needs is not sitting well with me.

Fighting a devious grin, he gives a hard tug and rips off my lace panties. They shred to his whim and are stuffed into his jacket pocket.

I stare up at him in disbelief, and if I'm honest, a bit pissed off. "Those were my favorite panties. I would've taken them off for you. You didn't have to go all caveman on me and rip them!"

He smiles with amusement at my temper, which only heightens it. "Hush, Jessica. What's done is done. If it'll make you happy and stop you from frowning, then I promise to buy you more later. Now lie back down so I can taste you."

At a loss for words, I keep my mouth shut and nod mutely.

Without hesitation, Alex uses his knee to spread my legs wide apart while holding my gaze captive with his. My face flames red. I want to look away from him and hide, but for some stupid reason, I can't seem to force my eyes to look away from him. This position has me completely exposed and far more vulnerable than I like. I watch him closely as he lowers his head. His tongue darts out as he licks me from ass to clit.

The sensation has me involuntarily bucking against his mouth. Releasing my hands, he grips my hips and holds them down as he repeats the motion. I throw my head back on a moan and fist my hands in his hair as my core tingles. Using the pad of his thumb, Alex runs small circles over my throbbing clit as he slips a single digit inside of me. I rock my hips against his motions, enjoying the way his hands and mouth are working together to bring me pleasure.

"You're so tight, baby," he growls with approval.

"I want to come, Alex," I beg as my body trembles and aches for more. "I'm so close."

He smiles up at me. "You will, my love, but only when I'm ready for you too."

His magical tongue licks up and down my wet folds, tasting me as his tongue does things that make my body quake with awareness. I shamelessly moan like a hooker as he works his finger in and out of me, properly fingerfucking me as he trades one finger for two. Clenching my teeth, I grasp the leather seat with my hands, trying unsuccessfully to ground my emotions and steady myself.

I feel my orgasm building. Something within me is responding to this man in a way I never have with another. I tilt my hips up, trying to find the friction I need to throw myself over, but being the bastard he is, Alex continues to hold me down, not giving me an inch of leverage.

"Do you like my mouth on you, baby? Do you want me to suck that lovely clit of yours?"

I nod my head. I anticipate the heat of his mouth on me but instead get nothing. Nothing. No, mouth. No, fingers. No movement at all. Confused, I lift my head and glare at his prone body through blurry eyes. Swallowing hard, I ask the million-dollar question. "Why the hell did you stop?"

"I want to hear you say it. Tell me what you need. Don't nod your head at me. If you want me to suck on your pussy and lick every drop of your juices from you, then you need to say it."

I roll my eyes in irritation. I've never been good at dirty talk. But my arousal has turned near painfully, so pushing my insecurities aside, I do as he requests. "Mr. Harlow, please stop being a dickhead and put your magical tongue on me for Christ's sake. I need to feel you licking me."

With a chuckle and a twist of his wrist, he thrusts his fingers deep within my channel and curls his fingers in a come here motion while stroking his tongue roughly against my clit. It's the perfect combination and gives me that extra push I needed.

Fisting my hands in his hair, I hold on for dear life as my body trembles with the beginning of a very powerful orgasm. Throwing my head back, I scream out as my senses go into overload. It's the most incredible and intense feeling. With my legs clamped around his head, holding him to me, he continues to lick me, easing me down as the waves slowly decrease, and my body stops trembling.

Blinking my eyes open, I find Alex hovering over me. He watches me with a small smile on his lips. I'm exhausted. It takes a moment for the realization that we're still in the limo to hit me. I glance towards the partition and silently pray that his driver didn't hear me. I cover my face in shame; he probably did.

Sensing my apprehension, Alex captures my gaze. "Don't worry about it. This area is soundproof. Even if he were able to hear anything, he would never acknowledge it. All my employees sign a confidentiality agreement before working for me."

"Oh...So, you do this often?" I inquire, a sick feeling churning in my gut.

I always choose the playboys. When will I ever learn?

"No, Jessica. I don't make a habit of picking up a beautiful woman and driving them to climax in the back of my limo." He laughs as he pulls his shirt back on. I lick my parched lips watching him adjust his rock-hard erection.

I'm too tired to speak, so I just nod. Uncomfortable with my lack of clothing, I sit up follow Alex's lead and begin re-dressing, minus the panties of course. The crazy bastard still has them stuffed in his jacket pocket. Ten minutes later we pull into the parking garage at *Glimmer Magazine*.

My head tilts in the barest nod in confusion as I stare up at the building. Moving in a fluid motion, Alex slips out of the car and stands with an outstretched hand towards me.

Taking his hand, I ask the question stuck to the tip of my tongue. "Why are we at your office?"

Alex stares at me for a second, giving me a funny look. "This is where I live. When I took over the magazine from my mom, I transformed the top level into a penthouse. I can't wait for you see it."

Retrieving my bagged dinner from Carlson, he leads me through the glass front-entry doors and steers me toward the elevator banks with his hand planted firmly on the small of my back. The mere touch re-ignites a burn deep in my belly.

Ushering me into the waiting elevator, I wait against the car wall, while he pushes the button P—obviously for the penthouse—and scans his security card over a black panel. Nervous flutters take flight in my stomach, erupting into chaos the closer we ascend to our destination.

Get a grip, Jess. He just went down on you in a limo; sex should be a piece of cake after that.

The elevator door opens to a large expansive entryway with white marble floors and high ceilings. Ushering me inside, Alex leads me to into what looks to be the main room. The sound of my heels clicking against the marble resonates throughout the room, indicating just how large it is. I take a moment appraise my surroundings.

The place is simple in design. Walls have been removed to create open and naturally lighted spaces, with elegant touches and modern furniture throughout. Not that I would expect anything less. The decor is classy yet reserved with a palette of dark grays, ivory, and touches of gold thrown in. Dark wood furnishings, soft leather sofas, modern art, and high-end decorative elements bring the whole place together. It is masculine, but not in a tacky, or bachelor pad type of way. The back wall is the masterpiece that brings it all together. The entire wall, from top to bottom, is made of glass with a copycat view of downtown Dallas that you see from his office a few floors down.

It is all breathtaking and so very not me. I sigh as I glance at the sight of the glittering city lights in the distance. His whole place screams sophistication and money where my home shouts comfort with a side of homemade mac and cheese.

"Your home is gorgeous." I can't get over the size of it. You could fit my whole apartment in the living room alone. What does one person do with so much space?

He gives me a small smile before leaning in and delivering me a sweet kiss. "Thanks. I am glad you like it." His voice is sincere and sounds pleased.

I track his movements as he walks through the rooms, flipping on lights and encasing the whole place in a soft, light glow. I watch with delight as he shrugs out of his suit jacket and tie before tossing them over a nearby chair. No matter how small the task, Alex moves with purpose and confidence.

Turning back around, he catches me ogling his backside and a smile tugs at his lips. "See something you like, Ms. Grayson?"

"Maybe," I answer, a flush spreading over my cheeks. I feel so out of my element around him. It's slightly uncomfortable, but not enough to send me running for the hills. At least, not yet.

Taking my hand, he leads me to the kitchen. I am not a big cook. I can make a mean lasagna, but that is the extent of my expertise. That being said, even a rookie like me can appreciate a kitchen such as his. It's a freaking chef's wet dream.

The same color palette continues throughout the area. What catches my attention right away are the long, gray, marble countertops, an enormous island with built-in wood chopping boards, and commercial-grade, stainless steel appliances. Studying the room, I can't help but wonder if he does any cooking here himself, or if he has someone on staff who does it for him. Probably the later.

"Sit," he commands, motioning to one of the bar stools at the end of the breakfast bar. "Try and relax while I warm up your dinner."

I scrunch up my nose. Despite how hungry I was earlier, the idea of food has now lost its appeal, and I tell him as much.

"You need to keep your strength up for later," he says, flashing me a panty-dropping grin.

Seeing him move around the kitchen with ease is a bit shocking and a whole lot of sexy. I would never have pegged him as the type of man who would even know how to operate a microwave, let alone an oven or stove.

I glance at said stove and wonder what all the buttons encasing the front of it do. Mine at home has only a single dial for adjusting the temperature and one button for the interior light. Why would a person need anything more?

"Is water okay? Or would you prefer something else? I've got a white wine that would go nicely with Italian food." Alex's light voice draws me out of my head.

"Oh, um...water works for me."

I struggle to find something interesting to converse about. Even the simplest of small talk is evading me at the moment. The realization that I don't know anything about Alex is daunting. I have to remind myself that this was my idea. This is what I wanted.

He and I are not a couple nor are we dating. What we have is strictly about pleasure. It's a healthy way for me to exorcise him from my thoughts. Asking him personal questions or trying to get to know him is pointless.

I keep telling myself that over and over, hoping if I think it enough times, I might trick myself into believing it.

Alex hums quietly. "You're doing it again, babe."

"Huh?" I ask, my brows furrowed. "Did you say something?" It's mortifying I can't seem to keep it together whenever he is around. It's as if my brain disconnects the minute we connect.

He paused to peer into my eyes, the weight of them on me causing me to fidget. "Stop overthinking everything. It's just you and me here. There is no right or wrong, good or bad. You get me?"

Swallowing hard, I nod a shaky yes.

Placing a warm, heaping plate of my spaghetti in front of me, along with a glass of ice water, Alex takes a seat beside. "Eat," he orders. "You will feel better once you have something in your stomach."

Not wanting to be rude, I dig into my food, taking small bites in hope of keeping most of the sauce in my mouth and not all over my face. I manage to get a small portion of my dinner eaten. The majority of it ends up being pushed around my plate like I did back when I was a kid and didn't want to eat my vegetables. Alex does not appear amused. My mother never was either. She used to scold me countless times for wasting food. Then again, there wasn't much that I could do that didn't upset my mom.

Standing, I help clear the table, making sure the kitchen is spotless and pristine once again. With nerves swirling relentlessly in my tummy, I follow him back into the living room with the expectation we will retire to the bedroom and pick back up where we left off in the car earlier.

Except that is not what happens. Alex catches me off guard by walking over to an elaborate speaker system near the entry way and keys in entries on an iPod. When "Made for You" by One Republic, begins streaming through the penthouse speakers, his heated emerald orbs turn my way.

I swallow hard seeing the desire blanketing his face. He wants me, and I can't deny feeling the same way about him. My breath catches when he grabs my hand and yanks me against his hard frame. His hard erection fits snuggly against my cleft as we move to the music.

I bit back a groan and press closer to him. *I love this song.*

My emotions are all over the place as I try to understand the complexity of this man. One minute he is demanding and controlling, and the next he is gentle and charismatic. His mood swings are worse than Jane when she has a bad case of PMS. Trust me when I say that's not a pretty sight.

"What are you thinking?" he asks, his breath tickling my ear.

My head is lying on his chest. My hand is holding his while his other hand is wrapped around my waist, as we sway to the music. Listening to the lyrics of the song, I can't help but wonder if we could make it work between us. Having anything more with him feels like a fantasy and one that scares the hell out of me. "You confuse me," I confess. My voice is so light I wonder if he heard me.

I don't dare look up at him. Every time I look into his face, I feel like I am losing a piece of myself, and that is not something that can happen. *Not ever again.*

The air around us is thick and that familiar electric charge that manifests every time we touch is back with a vengeance. Still dancing, he kisses my forehead and lets out a heavy sigh. I can tell he wants to say something but for the first time tonight seems to be picking his words carefully.

"I won't pretend that I'm easy to deal with," he murmurs into my ear. "I like to be in control of things and don't react well when I'm not."

I roll my eyes. "So I've noticed."

He growls against my skin, and a delicious shiver travels down my spine. "I've been called a prick and much worse. And that is by people that like me," he chuckles. "I'm demanding and relentless when I go after something I want." His head pulls back, and his eyes bore into mine, holding me captive. "I want you, Jessica. All of you and nothing less."

My breath catches in my throat. *Me?* I wait for a beat, thinking he is going to say more, but he remains silent.

"What does that mean?" I gently probe. I have a feeling I'm not going to like his answer, but that does not stop me from wanting to hear it.

My feet falter as our dancing ends. I lean into his sturdy frame, needing the security he is providing to stay upright. The last thing I need is to turn into a puddle of goo on the floor. He chuckles softly, never missing the effect he has on me.

"I'm not going to apologize for who I am. I need to be in charge—complete control, in and out of the bedroom. I don't know how to be anything else. I promise not to hurt you. Your pleasure is my first concern. Always."

I study his face, but his stoic features aren't giving off anything. His brows are lifted, and it's then that I see it. His eyes are the key to his feelings. They betray him, showing a storm of emotions brewing closely under the surface.

"I won't try and change you, Alex. Hell, it's not my place to do so even if I desired to. You don't have to explain yourself to me," I say honestly.

Raking a hand through his gorgeous hair, he lets out an exasperated breath. "I swear, Jessica, if you say there is nothing more than sex between us again, I'll take you over my knee and spank you."

I snort with laughter. *Spank me? Surely he is joking.* I adopt a calming breath as I regroup, needing to try and regain the upper hand.

"You agreed earlier when I offered you sex with no strings attached. I never promised to become anything more to you." Ignoring his narrowed eyes, I continue to babble on. "You and I are bad for each other. I'm not inclined to play games. Been there, done that, not going back."

My voice sounds calm despite the raging anger brewing within. I told myself that being around him would be a bad idea and instead of holding to my principles, I let my hormones rule me, and now I'm in over my head. *Stupid, fucking hormones.*

His jaw clenches to the point that I'm afraid it might snap. I take a cautious step back. I don't know Alex well enough to understand what he is thinking or how he will react.

Alex works his jaw as his gaze cuts through me. He appears to be contemplating something, what I have no clue.

My heart beats harder as a smoldering smile crosses his lips. The electricity crackles hot between us once again.

Alex rocks back on his heels, his hands sliding into his pant pockets. "I lied," he replies, a slow twitch tipping his lips. "You can try and run after tonight, but understand that I will always be one step ahead of you. You're under my skin, baby. I can't get enough of you, and I don't think I want to.

"I plan to consume you. I will fuck that sweet, little body of yours over and over, and when I'm done with you, you will be *mine*. Every fucking inch of you will beg for my cock. Mind, body, and soul. I'm claiming you, Jessica." He levels his heated gaze on me.

He is challenging me to disagree, and Lord help me, I know I need to speak up, but fuck me sideways, I'm speechless.

By the time I find my voice, it's too late. Alex is in front of me and grabbing at my waist as he releases a low, frustrated growl. I'm yanked up against him as his hand grips the nape of my neck. My hormones kick into gear as his mouth hovers over mine, our breaths mingle for a second before his mouth claims mine. The kiss is as wild and uncontrolled as he is.

His tongue slips past my lips to dance with my own. He tastes divine, a flavor consisting of cinnamon and vanilla that I will never tire of.

Pulling and tugging, our bodies grind against each other in reckless abandonment. His encased hard-on grinds against me, hitting my clit in the most exquisite way. I rock my hips forward, wanting more as I need a way to snuff out the fire burning in my core. Our hurried movements, remind me of horny teenagers going at it before their parents get home. I can't remember the last time I felt this alive.

My head falls back as he continues to explore my body using his hands and mouth. With nimble fingers, Alex works at shedding my clothes, leaving me standing in only my lace bra. The chilled air rushes over my body making me shiver.

Damn, I wish I still had my panties. They might not have been much more than a thin scrap of material, but even that is better than nothing at all.

Ignoring my unease, Alex licks his lips. My eyes track the movement, remembering the delicious pleasure his talented tongue brought me earlier. An embarrassing moan slips out, and I duck my head to keep my heated cheeks from showing.

Alex chuckles, apparently hearing the sound and catching onto the dirty track my mind has detoured to. "I'm going to enjoy feasting on every inch of your sweet body, baby."

I bit my lip to keep from moaning again. Stepping into my space, Alex moves his arms around me. His hand loops into my bra strap and with a flick of his talented fingers, releases the clasp open, allowing the straps to fall over my shoulders and onto the floor.

I'm not self-conscious about my body. I work out and do my part to keep fit and healthy, but being completely naked, while his hooded eyes drink me in is unnerving at best.

"You are so beautiful," he murmurs.

Entwining a hand in my hair, Alex gives it a tug, causing my face to tilt up, and allowing him free access to my mouth and exposed neck. I inhale a sharp breath as his lips slant against mine. His tongue sweeps across the crease of my lips, and I open, giving him the access he needs to deepen the kiss. He doesn't hesitate as his tongue slips in, caressing me with soft, languid strokes. The sounds of our pleasure resonate in the empty room.

With every stroke of his tongue, my resolve melts away. If it weren't for his hand around my waist holding me up, I would be flat on my ass by now. My knees are the consistency of jelly and proving worthless at keeping me vertical.

Dipping my head to the crook of his neck, I trace my nose along his skin before lightly running my teeth against the delicate patch behind his ear. His pulse jumps, the throbbing flesh pounds against my mouth, beating a staccato that matches the one hammering away in my core.

With a groan, Alex cups my ass and lifts me into his arms. On instinct, I wrap my legs around his waist, sealing our bodies together as my arms entwine around his neck. I hold on tight as he begins to walk, carrying me to what I can only hope is his bedroom.

Leaving the lights at a soft glow, we climb onto the bed, still fused together. Both of us refusing to release our hold on the other. The crisp linens are a welcome contrast to my feverish skin. I lick my lips as his hand travels the length of my body, landing solidly on my most intimate part. My head is spinning as his fingers slide through my wet folds, his touch light, and teasing.

"I want you naked," I groan, my hips shifting on their own as my legs part for him.

Pulling away he stands and shucks off his clothing. My eyes roam his body, taking him in and appreciating everything I see. There is just enough light in the room to give me a glorified view of his well-muscled torso and beautifully sculpted hips. My eyes latch onto his thick cock and my body clenches in anticipation of what's to come.

Dressed, Alex is handsome. Naked, Alex is magnificent. He is the holy grail of men. I lick my lips in want, remembering the taste of him in my mouth and the feel of him stretching me.

"It's fucking hot when you look at me like that," he mutters.

"How am I looking at you?" I ask coyly.

"Like you want to devour me," he groans. Keeping his eyes locked with mine, his hand wraps around his cock, and he begins a slow stroking motion. My eyes zero in on the bead of moisture coating the tip. I moan in appreciation as my mouth waters to taste him once again.

"So why are you still standing there?" I question with an arched brow. "Get your tight ass over here and let me have what I want." I lick my lips to moisten them as I stare unabashedly at his thickening cock.

I get a sexy growl in return for my effort. Placing a knee on the bed, Alex crawls back up the bed, licking and nibbling my body in the process. My body heat rises in response to his closeness. The closer he gets to my breasts, the harder they become. My peaks stand at attention, begging for the slightest touch.

Alex does not disappoint as he takes the sensitive nipple into his warm mouth. Latching onto it, his tongue whirls around, making it hard as ice while sucking on it greedily.

Lacing my hands around his neck, I curl my fingers into his hair and buck up against him grinding my clit against his erection as I try and seek some much-needed relief. The contact heightens my desire, but it is not enough to push me over. If anything it only frustrates me further.

"Alex, I need more," I breathe against his lips. I rub my hips against his to help get my point across.

"I can help with that," he responds, his teeth grazing the curve of my neck.

Reaching a hand down between our sweaty bodies, he slips one finger into my drenched channel while his thumb rubs firm circles on my throbbing clit. It's the perfect combination and within a matter of minutes, I'm falling off the proverbial cliff. Throwing my head back, I scream out as my body quakes and splinters off into a million glorified pieces.

"That's it, baby," Alex growls. "Come for me, Jessica. Paint my fingers with your cum."

My head slams back into the blankets as I chant his name over and over like a fucking song. As the haze from my orgasm subsides, I blink my eyes open to find Alex staring down at me with a lazy grin.

Slipping his fingers out of my pussy he brings them to his mouth, and with his gaze holding me prisoner, he places them in his mouth and licks them clean of my essence.

"You taste like heaven, baby," he says, his voice soft and sultry.

Holy fuckbuckets, that was hot! I groan out a few unintelligible sounds while trying to cover my overheated face.

Leaning forward, I press my lips to his. While he is distracted, I take the opportunity, one of the few I will probably ever get, and wrap my legs around his hips in an effort to take control. I roll him off me and on his back, using the momentum to pull myself up, so I am now straddling him. Catching the surprised look on his face, I can't squelch the laugh that bubbles up.

Before I lose my nerve, I reach down and grip his hard shaft, fisting my hand tightly around it. Smiling at his sharp intake of breath, I move my hand up and down, stroking him thoroughly with a firm grip. Alex throws his head back as my thumb flicks over the plump crown, and I give it a gentle squeeze. A satisfied moan rips from his chest as I continue to work his cock with one hand while massaging his balls with the other.

With lips parted, he peers up at me through slitted eyes. "You need to stop, gorgeous. I don't want to come in your hand or on your tits. I want to save that experience for your tight pussy."

His words are my undoing. Heat unfurls through my body as I tremble with arousal. "Fuck me, Alex. I want to feel you inside of me," I plead.

Flipping me onto my back, Alex reaches into the bedside table drawer and pulls out a foil package. Ripping it open, he grips his cock firmly in one hand as he rolls the condom over his hard length. I lick my lips, wishing I had taken the time earlier to taste him when I had the chance. Stroking his sheathed cock, Alex hovers over me and flexes his hips while trying to keep the bulk of his weight off me.

I lean up and press my lips against his as I wrap my arms around his neck, needing more contact. I love the feel of his skin sliding against mine. With a shift of his hips, he guides his cock to my pussy, rubbing the tip against my opening as he coats himself in my wetness. I close my eyes and bite back a moan as I open my legs wider, giving him full access. My head pressed into the pillow, I shut my eyes and try to lose myself in the sensations coursing through me. It has been far too long since I've gotten my freak on, and every touch and shift of his body against mine fuels the wildfire running through my veins.

"Stay with me, Jessica," Alex barks out, the harshness in his voice unnerves me.

My eyes snap open and lock with his angered ones. I shake my head as I try and decipher why the hell he's pissed.

"Don't you dare close your eyes on me. Watch me make you come. Feel my cock claiming you. Stop acting as if this is nothing but another casual fuck. This isn't just sex, baby," he rasps through his teeth.

Not breaking our gaze, I huff loudly, the sound resonating in the quiet room. "Don't ruin this for me, Alex," I warn, my own ire surfacing. "Pillow talk can happen later. Now, please shut up and fuck me before I decide to take matters into my own hands and leave you to do the same."

Without warning, Alex grips my hips with bruising force and plunges into me. His hardness and thick girth spear into me with a force that has me crying out. He stills inside of me, holding firm and giving my body a chance to acclimate to his size. Sliding out to the tip, Alex stills above me, his body refusing to move.

I blink in confusion. What is he waiting for?

His lips turn up as he studies me. What he says next has me seeing stars. "I need to hear it," he says, his voice soft, yet commanding. "Tell me you want more. I don't want just a fuck toy, Jess. I can get that anywhere, and it doesn't appeal to me."

My chest feels heavy like someone is pressing down on it. I frown. The idea of him with someone else leaves a bad taste in my mouth. I don't do jealousy well, and despite my objections to us being a couple, I can feel it surfacing.

He rests his forehead against mine and holds my attention." I know you're scared, babe, but I swear I won't hurt you," he says his voice a sensual purr. "Agree to something more. We don't have to label it, but I need to know that you won't disappear on me after tonight."

I bite my bottom lip as I stare up into his beautiful face. It's not that I don't feel something for Alex because I do, but being put on the spot freaks me out, and I hate being forced into anything. Tightening my legs around him, I try to buck up my hips and make him take me again, but being the bastard he is, he just pulls further back. With my greedy body burning with need, my resolve quickly melts.

Pushing aside my pride, I do the one thing I am sure to regret later. I give in. "All right," I say, my voice shaky. "I want you. I want your cock in me and I want as many orgasms as you can give me. I promise to continue this for as long as it works for the both of us." Leaning up, I brush my lips against his, seeking the access I need to plunge my tongue into his mouth, deepening the kiss until we are both left breathless and panting.

My mind is left spinning. How in the hell am I going to end this when the time comes?

Without any hint of hesitation, he slams back into me, grinding his hips in a semi-circle before pulling back out and repeating the motion. I clench my hands in the sheets around me to keep from squirming, my body already on the brink of unraveling.

"Damn, baby, you're so tight and warm. You feel fucking incredible," he grunts as he pounds into me. Leaning forward, I capture his nipple in my mouth and suck it greedily, rasping my teeth against the tight nub. His body shudders, and I can't help the smile blooming on my face.

"Damn, Jessica. You drive me crazy," he gasps.

I love that I have this effect on him. Watching the confident and controlled Alex fall apart in my hands is a powerful thing, a feeling that could become an addiction if left unchecked.

I watch his muscular thighs as his hips rock into me. His thrusts are slow and steady as his hands cup my ass, keeping the motion controlled. The combined smell of sex in the air and the sound of skin slapping against skin has wetness pooling between my legs. His teeth graze my neck as his fingers move to my breasts, exploring my nakedness, as his cock flexes against my clit. A desperate moan slips from my lips as my body clings to his; the need to come overwhelms me in the best of ways.

"Your pussy is heaven, baby. Fuck yourself on my cock. Take what you need." He presses in deeper, his full length touching me in places no one had dared to reach. The sensation is mind-blowing, but the slow pace he's using is keeping my orgasm from progressing.

I love his filthy words. No one has ever spoken to me that way and although it might be wrong; I find it sexy. Sweat pours from my quivering body as Alex takes my mouth. His tongue lashes in an aggressive way that has me seeing stars.

Pulling free from his hold, I glare at him through hooded eyes. "I need to come, you dirty bastard." My nails rake down his back as I try and urge him to take me harder. I don't care if I walk funny tomorrow as long as I get off and leave here a happy woman.

Dark green eyes hold me in place. "What's stopping you?"

"You, asshole," I deadpan, giving him my best scowl. "I need it harder. Slow and sweet might feel like heaven, but tonight I need more. Stop being a tease, and fuck me like you mean it."

He laughs, the sound deep, dangerous, and a complete contrast to the smile he wears. "Say it, baby," he urges, his voice rough. He lazily drives into me, keeping the fire in my core stoked, but contained. "Say you're my girl, and I will fuck your sweet flesh until it's so sore you'll feel me long after this night is over."

I absorb his words as I bite back the plentitude of obscenities that run through my mind. There is no getting out of this, not unless I want to walk away from here pissed off, horny, and unappeased. Steeling my spine, I tell him what he wishes to hear. "I'm yours, Alex. All yours," I say, my voice soft but confident in my conviction.

Smiling like the cat that ate the cream, he drops a kiss onto the shell of my ear. "I know," he murmurs, his silky voice skating over my body like a live wire. Grabbing my legs, he positions them over his shoulders, before guiding his cock back into my greedy pussy. "I want you to come for me, baby. Bathe my cock in your cum," he moans. His hips retreat a moment before hammering back into me with a force that leaves me lightheaded.

His strokes are brutal and with the way his hands are gripping my hips, I am sure to see bruises tomorrow, but I don't care. The pleasure that had been building all night is reaching a crescendo. With a loud scream, I throw my head back and take what I need until I shatter. The world disappears around me as my pussy clenches around his swollen cock, milking it for all its worth.

"Christ, baby," he rasps. His grip on my legs tightens as he slams into me once, twice, three times before shuddering over me and finding his own release.

We collapse in a tangle of limbs, as we both struggle to calm our ragged breathing. With a raised hand, Alex sweeps a stray strand of hair behind my ear. I lean into his touch as I glance up at him through my lashes. My mind feels like it's on a roller coaster, riding the ups and downs of my emotions while I struggle to define where we go from here.

Alex lets out a long sigh as his lips brush my temple. "Don't overthink it, baby. For one night try and shut off that overactive mind of yours."

I blink up at him. "How do you do that?" I ask amazed at his Spidey senses. "How in the hell do you always know what I'm thinking? You barely know me."

Ignoring my question, he slides out of me and heads to the bathroom to dispose of the condom. I stretch out my body and cuddle into the sheets, allowing my tired eyes a chance to rest finally. The last several days have depleted me mentally and emotionally, and now thanks to Alex, physically as well.

Moments later I feel the bed dip behind me right before I'm surrounded by a mountain of muscle. There is a lot that needs to be said between us, but for once I am too tired to continue to delve further into the do's and don'ts that define us. There is always tomorrow for that.

Pulling the blanket further around us, I curl into his chest and fall fast asleep.

Chapter Seven

Hearing the shrill ring of a phone, I blink my bleary eyes open to find myself...alone.

It takes me a moment or two to remember where I am and how I got here. I blush as the memory of last night hits me. If the soreness in my body wasn't enough of a reminder of him, the elegant decor and posh furnishings surrounding me are.

I finger a fuzzy tassel hanging from a pillow beside me with a snort. Don't get me wrong, everything around me is stunning, but it is so not my style. If there were ever an example of two people who are as different as night and day, Alex and I would be it.

I can't help but let my gaze wander around the room, checking out the lavish draperies, the perfectly positioned pictures on the wall, and the pristine furniture. Everything looks brand, spanking new. We came in here in such a whirlwind last night; I never had the chance to scope out his bedroom.

A person's bedroom can tell a lot about an individual. Right now this one is saying that Alex paid a very knowledgeable interior designer to decorate this room and probably has a small army of maids keeping it this clean. There is no way in a hell a man, not even one of his caliber, could put this color palette and perfection together and then never screw it up.

Stretching out in his bed, which feels larger than any king bed I have ever been in, I wince at the persistent ache attacking my muscles. I let out a dreamy sigh, as vivid images of Alex pounding into my needy pussy infiltrate my dirty mind. I am so screwed where he is concerned. Alex is a weakness I don't need, and one I can see becoming a problem for me. The bastard is my very own kryptonite.

I yank a pillow over my face and let out a silent scream. *Get a grip Jess. No amount of orgasms is worth this.*

Or are they?

Chill snakes down at my naked body. I search the room for my clothes but come up empty. Not knowing where Alex is or who else could be in his home, I began opening drawer after drawer, looking for something to cover myself with. I settle on a large t-shirt and silk boxers, which I have to roll down twice just to keep them on my hips. Not the best look for my small frame, but it does the job.

As I head toward the door, out of the corner of my eyes, I take notice of the numbers highlighted on an alarm clock beside the bed. All air leaves me as panic seizes my chest. *I fucking overslept.* My tired brain bursts to life as I calculate how much time I need. If I leave now, and the traffic gods shined upon me, clearing away all slow cars on the roadways, I could make it home with minutes to spare, allowing me just enough time to shower and dress. Last night, I promised Jane I would drive to work with her, and after my disappearing stunt from the restaurant, I can't afford to flake out on her again.

I run my fingers through my hair, trying to comb through my mass of tangles to shape my mussed mane into something manageable. It's days like these I wish Jane's OCD about being prepared by always having a large purse filled with emergency products and knickknacks on hand would rub off on me. I would kill for a comb and a toothbrush right about now.

I pad silently into the living room, past the kitchen, and into a new section of the house I bypassed last night in my search for food and mind blowing sex. I follow the sound of Alex's voice until I come to what I assume to be his office. The door is slightly ajar, and from my vantage point in the hall I can make out a large desk, a wall of books, and a couple of couches. I watch Alex as he paces back and forth behind his desk with the phone stuck to his ear in what appears to be an important conversation.

My fingers skim the surface of the door, ready to knock and grab Alex's attention in hopes that his driver might be available to take me home. My hand halts mid-knock when I hear his voice escalate to what can only be considered a hostile tone. The fine hairs on the back of my neck prick with unease as I pick up bits and pieces of the heated, yet one-sided conversation.

I'm not normally one who makes a habit of eavesdropping on others, but being so close, Alex's words are loud and impossible to ignore. I keep out of sight and listen on, thinking I might be able to wait him out and still get some help on getting home.

Oh, hell who am I kidding? I'm curious about who and what he is talking about, and yes, I am sticking my nose into business that is none of mine. There I admitted it. I never claimed to be a Saint so you can't hold it against me.

"Unless you want me to stomp you into the ground and make you regret ever having the balls to pick up the phone and call me, you will leave her out of this." Alex yells every word, his tone clipped and harsh.

Being as quiet as possible, I take a step forward to get a better look into the room. Alex's pacing is enough to make me dizzy. His free hand tugs at his mussed hair while his other grips the phone tight enough that I hear the plastic cracking. His body turned back my way, I take a quick step back into the shadows.

"This is the only warning you will get, Lexy. I want our original agreement amended. My lawyers will be contacting you this week, and if you know what is good for you, you'll stop stalling. Our initial agreement is outdated. Stay out of my personal life, and I will do the same with yours. Who I fuck is none of your concern. The fact you're sneaky around and digging into my business makes you pathetic."

Lexy? Who is the her who needs to be left out of whatever they are speaking about, and who the hell is Lexy? Alex's words send ominous shivers through me. I never thought I would be the only woman he would be banging, but hearing him speak of fucking someone else makes me feel ill...and dirty. *I'm more than ready for that shower now.*

Knowing my limited time is dwindling to practically nothing, I weigh my options and make a judgment call. I need to get home. Running back into the living room, I search the area and locate my clothes neatly folded on the back of the sofa. Scooping them up along with purse and shoes, I make a dash for the front door.

Hitting the call button, I let out a sigh of relief when the doors open and the elevator car is readily available. As I descend, I pull out my phone and hit the speed-dial button I've programmed for a local taxi company I've used a time for two. While doing a funny balancing act of trying to get my shoes on, I talk to the all-too-cheery girl on the phone and request a cab. With luck still on my side, the company confirms they have one in the area, and assures me it will be will be rolling up within the next five minutes.

I know there is a chance that Alex is going to be upset when he finds I left without saying goodbye, but I will have to deal with his wounded ego later. Time away from him is the smart choice. It will give me time to think and figure out what is going on between us.

Is there even an *us* to figure out? Last night was intense and way more emotional than I expected.

Truthfully, he should be thanking me. Now, neither of us has to deal with the whole awkward, morning-after scenario. I hate those. The worst is when you just stare at each other, not knowing if you should hug goodbye, shake hands, or try and get in one more quickie before the spell is broken, and reality kicks you in the ass.

A small voice in the back of my mind is calling me a coward. Jane calls that voice the voice of reason. Whatever it is, it's ruining my good mood. I understand that running away from Alex won't solve my problems, but it's too late to change that now. What's done is done.

Stepping out of the elevator doors, a smile crosses my lips at finding the entry way empty of employees apart from the lone security guard I spotted last night on our way up. I flush as I walk past him in my walk of shame clothes. I'm sure he sees it often, but that does not curb the heat hitting my cheeks. Hurrying outside, I run to the curb where I find my cab waiting for me.

The cab driver keeps stealing glances at me. I think my choice of clothing or lack of it humors him. I'm thankful when he doesn't ask any questions and keeps his comments to himself. Rattling off my address, I rest my head on the back seat and shut my eyes.

Taking deep, controlled breaths, my mind races as it tries to come to grips with everything that happened last night. I don't regret the sex. Far from it. Sex with Alex is a treat and one any woman would welcome with open legs.

So why do I feel like I just made a pact with the devil?

****

Rushing into my apartment, I stop momentarily to give Jane a quick hello, before sprinting to the shower. My phone has been ringing nonstop since my cab pulled away from his place. I keep hitting the ignore button, refusing to take the call, but Alex is not taking the hint.

I waste no time washing away any remnants of my tryst from last night. Hearing him talk about fucking someone else canceled out any notions I might have had of repeating what Alex and I did last night. Drying off, I throw on my favorite blue silk dress, match it with my silver slingback shoes, and top it off with a blue clutch bag. Since I won't be meeting up with any customers today, I keep my makeup light and pull my hair into a low ponytail. Giving myself a final once-over, I am pleased with the outcome and more than a little surprised I was able to pull it all together in time.

Joining Jane in the living room, I smile in gratitude as I take the cup of coffee and bagel smeared with cream cheese she hands off to me. Sitting at the table, I waste no time digging in.

Jane was grinning at me as she gestured to my annoying phone, the one that won't stop singing "Crazy." "What is that about? The damn thing won't shut up."

I shrug, not wanting to fess up just yet. "It's a long story." I want to leave it at that, but apparently Jane has other plans.

She paces the floor, waiting me out and making it clear she is not going to let me get away with a simple brush off. Finishing my breakfast, I take my old purse and transfer my things into my new clutch, all the while considering how much I want to share.

Glancing up, she's still watching me, the patience in her eyes dwindling. "You can have the short version," I concede, ready to get this over with so we can leave. "I agreed to have sex with Alex as long as that was all it was between us. Sex only, no emotions or promises for more."

Her eyes widen with intrigue. "So how was it? Did he rock your world?"

I hesitate before replying. "It was incredible. In fact, it was the best I've ever had, but somehow it turned into more than just sex. I wasn't expecting that, and now I'm having a problem dealing with it."

"What's to deal with?" she snorts. "Obviously you like him, at least enough to do the horizontal tango and come out smiling, and it sounds like he likes you. Why are you making this difficult?"

I push a few stray strands of hair behind my ear. "My mind turns to mush whenever I get around him. It's too much. He's too much. Plus, we live in entirely different worlds. With work finally taking off, I don't have time to go off playing sex kitten to the rich and famous." I struggle to keep the frustration from my voice.

Jane studies me for a few minutes, and I cringe, feeling like a science experiment she is trying to pick apart. Before I can begin to speak again, Jane is already shaking her head with a smile on her face while clapping her hands in delight. I stare at her in shock, not sure what she is going on about.

"He got under your skin," she giggles, jumping up and down like a kid hopped up on too much sugar. "It's about time someone broke through those thick walls you keep locked around that stone heart of yours."

I shake my head, feeling a headache coming on. "You don't get it," I shout. "I woke up late this morning and panicked. When I found him, he was on what seemed to be an urgent phone call, so instead of interrupting and letting him know I was leaving, I snuck out and called a cab."

Jane's face morphs into one of shock and horror. She looks downright sick by my admission. "Please tell me you have spoken to him since then and are not being petty and ignoring him? Is this why your phone won't shut up?"

I suck in a deep breath as my eyes seek refuge, landing on anything but my pissed off friend. "Please stop looking at me like that," I plead. "I know it was a stupid move, but in my defense, it was early, and I wasn't thinking too clearly at the moment. Alex is a lot to handle, and I have not decided if I am up for the challenge yet."

I glance down at my ringing phone and grimace. "He's called and texted nonstop since I left." I lay my head against the sofa cushion and bury my face, embarrassed by my behavior.

"If you're not ready to talk to him, then don't, but at least have the courtesy to text him back and let him know that you're okay. I don't want to sound like a cold bitch, but what you did was wrong on so many levels. Not to mention, you seem to have forgotten that this man has the power to obliterate or increase our business," she says, apparently miffed at my behavior.

Shit! I forgot that bit of info.

As always, her words hit home. I can feel the tears welling up in my eyes, threatening to spill over. I feel like a moron. I never thought past my personal issues to consider the business ramifications of my actions. I waved my coffee at her. "You're right. I'm sorry. I will text him now and fix this."

Squeezing her hand, I mutter another apology. "I never meant to put our business at stake. I promise never to let my stupid emotional baggage get the better of me again."

Retrieving my phone, I delete all twenty-three missed calls and six texts, before sending a return message of my own.

Me: I am sorry for leaving the way I did this morning.

My phone beeps back immediately with a reply.

Alex: Why did you run away?

Me: Needed to get home ASAP and you were busy on the phone. Did not want to interrupt.

Alex. Don't run away from me! Ever. I'm heading to a meeting. We will talk about this later. Stop ignoring my calls. Do I need to give you a reminder of how good we are together?

Me: No reminders needed.

Last time he reminded me, I ended up naked in the back of a limo.

"Is he still mad?" Jane inquires while searching through her bottomless pit of a purse for her keys. Finding them, she heads to the door, finally ready to go.

I shrug and grab my purse as I follow her out. "He is not exactly happy, but I think it will blow over. Catastrophe evaded."

The humid Texas air hits me like a freight train. In Texas, you get two types of heat, bearable and fry an egg on the sidewalk hot. Today is definably a fried egg kind of day. Choosing to wear silk was an ill thought out choice. The light material is already clinging to my body like a second skin. You can live in Texas your whole life and never get accustomed to the weather. I sure as hell haven't.

Climbing into her sleek Infinity, I crank up the radio and zone out, listening to some odd retro tune filtering through the speakers. Traffic is light this morning, and we arrive at work in record time. Walking into our building, I say a quick hello to Clive, before heading up to our place on the third floor. Clive is a gentle old man who works the security station.

He and I became good friends the first day we moved into the building. Clive has worked in the building for over fifteen years and calls almost everyone here by their first name. I always kid with him that he's one of the last true gentleman left in the world. Lorraine, his wife of over forty years, agrees with me.

Jane has two appointments scheduled for today. I purposefully left my day open so that I could get caught up on routine paperwork and inventory checks. I love my job and having my best friend as a business partner is the best. When we first opened our doors, business was slow and rocky at best, but it is steadily getting better due to some strategic advertising and word of mouth. Clients keep dribbling in on a consistent basis, but getting those customers to pay their invoices on time, has become a problem we were not anticipating. Hence the reason I am spending the day updating accounts and sending out late notices.

Lost in counting receipts, I jump when I hear the not-so-subtle cough of someone trying to gain my attention. Standing nervously in the doorway is a young man holding a large, white, pastry box in his hands. He fidgets from foot to foot, obviously out of his element and unsure of what he's doing.

I glance down at the papers in my hand. *That makes two of us.*

"Sorry if I startled you. I've got a delivery for a..." he looks down at the card in his hands. "A Ms. Grayson." His voice cracks on my name.

My lips purse as my brows rise in question. "That would be me."

My body sways as I try to peer behind and around him to see what he's got with him, but besides the pastry box, his hands are empty.

"Oh great," the boy exclaims, practically throwing the box onto my desk. "These are for you. Have a great day."

Ignoring his sudden retreat, I stare down at the box in front of me, mildly confused and more than a little bewildered. Who sends pastries as a gift? There is a small envelope attached to the top that I quickly pull off and tear open. Inside the little pocket is a vanilla card embossed with the letters AH at the top. Smiling despite my trepidation, I read the card.

For the one who tried to get away. Never again. I'll be seeing you soon, my love.

xAH

What the hell? I hesitantly flip open the white box to find a dozen delicious donuts winking back at me. I moan as the scent of the warm, gooey, sugary icing hits my nose.

Donuts? He sent me a dozen donuts.

I don't think I will ever be able to look at a donut as a simple, yummy, high calorie treat again. Now every time I see one, I will think of Alex and the first time we met.

The rest of the day crawls by at a snail's pace. As boring as it is, I am thankful for the reprieve and the chance to get caught up on all the tedious work I've been putting off. Procrastination is a bitch, and it's also a bad habit I've never been able to break.

Still, no matter how many entries I make or how many cases of lip gloss I count, visions of emerald-green eyes and drool-worthy abs keep sneaking their way back into my thoughts. In a moment of weakness, I broke down and texted him. I blame it on the donuts.

I shouldn't have reached out to him, but I figured it was the least I could do. I might be a chicken when it comes to relationships, but I've got manners, and it would have been rude not to have thanked him for the gooey treat.

So imagine my disappointment when he never responded. At every ring and beep of my phone, I race to answer it, and each and every time I get more irate when I find someone else on the other end. One day of ignoring me wouldn't be so bad, but the rest of the week goes the same way. No amount of work has been able to distract me. By Friday, I'm beside myself and itching to do something. Anything that will help me feel normal again and not like some love-sick teenager with a serious crush.

Jane came back a little after lunch time from her last appointment of the day with a big smile on her face. To say she is excited would be putting it mildly. She's dancing around the office, looking more like a person getting electrocuted and proclaiming that we need to go out and celebrate.

It seems her meeting went well, and the lucky bitch was triumphant in securing a contract with a large theater company. They've agreed to use our services exclusively for all their plays and events over the course of a year. I don't know how she did it, but I'm proud of her. This is by far one of the largest and most prestigious contracts we've gotten this year. Lord knows we need this. I'm hoping it will help to alleviate some of the bills that have been piling up. New customers are a blessing and something our company will need more of to survive.

"How about we grab some margaritas tonight at Juan's? I can see if Jax would like to join us?" Jane asks while stealing another one of my donuts and stuffing it into her mouth.

"Sure. Sounds like a plan to me."

I'm working hard to sound happy, but unfortunately, my mind is off in la-la land. Nothing has helped to ease my discomfort. I can't stop wondering why the hell he has yet to respond to me. To my dismay, one night was not enough to suppress my need for him. It pisses me off he already has this power over me. It's insane. Every time I think about him, a nagging ache takes root between my legs.

After my horrible break up with Travis, I swore never to let another man control or hurt me the way he had. I thought I loved Travis, but looking back at it now, I can't honestly say it was real. I mean, is it possible to love someone who only loves themselves? I think I was caught up in the whirlwind of it all. Travis was rich, gorgeous, and could charm the pants off of a nun. He was what my mom called a real catch, and I fell hard for him. I went around town with my head held high, proud that he had chosen me out of all the girls constantly chasing him around.

We dated for eight months and were practically inseparable when he proposed to me one night out by the lake. I was ecstatic and wasted no time in preparing for our wedding.

All my close friends told me I was making a mistake; they said Travis was pure trouble.

I didn't listen. I was high on the feeling of being in love. I never witnessed that side of him until it was too late. One day, I was scheduled to go dress shopping with Jane, except at the last minute she got sick and had to cancel on me. Not wanting to sit around town by myself, I decided to surprise Travis at work with lunch. When I showed up at his office, dressed in only a trench coat and heels holding a picnic basket filled with all his favorites, I ended up being the one surprised.

Travis was busy.

So was his secretary.

He had her bent over his desk, her skirt hiked up around her waist while he fucked her from behind. He wasn't the least bit fazed when I walked in on them. Needless to say, I freaked out. A lot of what happened after that is a blur when I try and think back on it.

Jane says a person's mind will blank out parts of a bad experience as a way to help you cope. All I remember is the shrill sound of my voice echoing through the room as I screamed, damning them both to hell while tears, tinged black from my mascara, painted my face.

As humiliating as all that was, it got worse when the jackass began yelling at me for interrupting his afternoon screw, all the while never stopping his rapid thrusts or fondling of her breasts.

At some point during my meltdown, I must have dropped the picnic lunch I had. As I ran out of his office, I slid through globs of potato salad and sub sandwiches and ruined my new pair of red suede shoes.

Travis comes from a wealthy and connected family in our small town. No penny was spared when it came to covering up his indiscretion. It was scary how well they covered his tracks, created lies, and made me out to be a horrible fiancé who refused to satisfy her man. They had everyone feeling sorry for the bastard.

Travis was a portrayed as a devoted fiancé, afraid to break off our engagement due to concern for my welfare. His lies hurt, and no matter how much I denied them, the damage to my reputation was done. Three months later I found out through the grapevine that Travis had married his slut secretary, and the happy couple had a bundle of joy on the way.

Travis broke me. He shredded all my hope in happy endings. I even went as far as making a dart board in my room and used Cinderella's face as the target. By the end of the summer, I was a champion dart player.

The only good that came out of being with Travis was Jax. He was Travis's best friend and one of the few people who learned firsthand the truth of what happened. He and Jane stood by me through all the ugliness, and once we graduated college, the three of us stuck together. We became our own version of a family and moved away to start a new life in the big city of Dallas.

My relationship with Travis left a horrible taste in my mouth. He made me wary of rich and powerful men, which is why I can't find it in me to trust Alex. I have no problem screwing him, but that is where it ends. He's been trouble from the beginning, and he has yet to contradict my initial feelings about him.

Sitting back in my chair, I close my eyes and will myself to stop being affected by him. I can't stand this obsessive need I have for him. *Only him.*

With a shake of my head, I retrieve my purse and call out to Jane, telling her to lock up and meet me downstairs when she is done. Someway, somehow I am going to purge all remnants of Alex from my system. If it happens to take all night, a new man on my arm, and a bottle of tequila to do it—then so be it.

Chapter Eight

"One more round," Jax calls to Randy, our favorite bartender.

Randy acknowledges our request with a nod and goes about making more margaritas. I swear each time he makes them, they come out stronger than the last. I began seeing double after my second. With my third on its way, I'm not certain I'll be able to function on my own.

"I don't think I should have any more," I protest, waving my hand in the air for no apparent reason.

I'm ignored by my two best friends who seem to be handling their drinks like a pro. Me, not so much. I blink my eyes repeatedly, willing them to focus on the bleary images around me. I give up, realizing it's useless and instead plant my head on top of my folded arms, hoping it will help to steady my movements. It doesn't. I still feel out of sorts.

"Jax," I call out louder, determined to garner his attention.

"You can handle one more, baby doll," Jax promises. I try and shake my head no, but stop when my head feels too heavy to follow through with the motion. *Damn it, I'm already drunk.*

"So Jane here was telling me that you finally gave it up to that magazine guy you worked for. Spill, babe, I want to hear all about it," he says, giving me one of his signature winks. Those sexy winks of his have made plenty of panties drop in their time. I might be his best friend, but I am not immune to his charm. Knowing he snores louder than a broken muffler and never puts the toilet seat down—no matter how many times you remind him—are a few of the things that keep those charms of his from ruining our friendship.

"I'm pleased to hear that my messed-up sex life keeps you two entertained."

I give them both a mock scowl or at least I try. With my impaired motor skills, I'm sure it comes off looking more like the Joker's creepy smile from Batman. My aim at intimidation fails miserably as my two best friends fall against each other, laughing hard enough to catch several glances from other patrons.

I find myself staring at their giggling selves wishing I could feel half as chipper as they do. "You two sound like a pack of hyenas," I gripe, taking another sip of my drink to keep from saying more.

"Quite being a spoilsport," Jax orders. Reaching across the booth, he pulls me to his side, using our difference in height to tuck me up under his arm. He drops a kiss to my forehead as he maneuvers us, so I am staring up into his sweet face. "You've got to open up, baby doll. I know you're scared, but from the little Jane has told me and after seeing you two together at the club, I think this guy might be good for you. If nothing else, you finally got those cobwebs dusted out from between your legs."

My brows rise in defiance. "Cobwebs?" I shake my head, trying to eradicate all images of long-legged spiders and other nasty creepy crawlies from my alcohol induced brain. With a point of my finger in his face, I aim to set him straight. "You're wrong, Jax. Alex is controlling, stubborn, and as much as I like the sex, it isn't enough to keep me going down this road. I was stupid for even trying. That man will eat me for dinner and spit me out the next day. "

I grab my fresh drink from Randy and treat it like a shot, downing the majority of it in one gulp. It's not my brightest move, but with all this talk about Alex circling the table, I need help in drowning out all the emotions fighting to bubble to the surface. This drink is stronger than the last and burns as it goes down, making my eyes tear up as I let out a string of loud hacking coughs.

Through my watery vision I catch the knowing looks Jane and Jax keep throwing each other. I ignore them and change the subject.

"How are things with David?" I ask Jane. As much as I still secretly wish he would take a hike and give Jane a chance with someone better, I keep my opinions bottled up and try to be the friend she needs. I don't know what it is about him, but he gives off a bad vibe that makes me wary of him.

"As good as can be expected considering he is halfway around the world." She frowns, and it makes me want to track David down and rip his balls off for making her sad. Shifting in her seat, she tries to make excuses for him, none of which I am believing. "Work has gotten crazy for him, and he doesn't think he will be able to visit as often as we had first hoped. This is probably harder for him than it is for me."

"You've got us, baby," I reply, my words sounding more slurred than before. "Who needs a man when you've got friends like us?" Then to top it off and confirm just how sloshed I am, I begin singing the theme song for *The Golden Girls*, that one about being a good friend. If there was any question about my sobriety, it has been answered loud and clear. I am drunk.

After two rounds of singing, I choose to ignore everyone and everything around me and enjoy the blissful, numb feeling that is spreading through my body like wildfire. That last drink was the winner, throwing me over the edge into sweet oblivion. I sit in silence with my head leaning on the booth and my eyes closed as my two friends joke together and act up. I smile as they bicker on, sounding more like siblings than good friends.

The song "Crazy" screaming from my phone draws my attention, sending a slew of chills down my spine. Frowning, I reach into my purse and pull out my phone, handing it likes it's a cobra ready to strike me down at any second. I stare at his name as it blinks across the small screen and my finger wavers precariously over the buttons. *To answer or not to answer?* Taking a deep breath, I hit the accept button. "Good evening, Master of the Universe," I say in a sing-song tone.

"Where are you?" No hello or how are you. Instead, I'm greeted with a gruffness I don't appreciate. He's demanding again. My hackles rise. I roll my eyes, glad he is not here to catch me doing it. I take another sip of my drink before answering him with a question of my own. "Why do you care, Mr. Harlow?"

Alex mutters curses so low I can barely comprehend them. He is trying to assert his dominance over me, and I'm not having it tonight. I might like that shit in the bedroom, but that doesn't mean I'll put up with it all the time. The drinks have given me a sense of false courage, and I plan on using it to show him I'm not someone he can push around or intimidate.

The silence stretches between us for longer than necessary. If it weren't for his deep breathing through the phone, I would have thought he had hung up.

After what feels like forever he finally speaks again. "You sound drunk?"

His concerned voice washes over me, and I take in a labored breath in an attempt to keep my wits about me. I can handle an angry or dominating Alex easily, but a caring Alex is something I'm not prepared for. His change in attitude throws me for a loop.

Blinking slowly, I adjust myself in my seat and notice two sets of eyes glaring at me from across the booth. Jax and Jane seem as consumed by my conversation with Alex as I am. I shoot them a what-the-fuck look, but they brush it off and keep on eavesdropping. *Damn nosey friends.*

"I'm indulging in a drink or three. Nothing for you to be concerned with."

"Are you alone?" His voice is back to sounding irritated which only serves to fuel my inner bitch. How dare he question me? I am not his to question. One night of great sex does not give him the right to dictate my actions. I am a grown woman for fuck's sake.

I sigh and drop my face into my hand as I rub my tired eyes. "It doesn't matter if I am or not," I reply barely above a whisper.

"When I ask you a question, Jessica, I expect an answer. An honest one. No bullshit." Alex pauses and lets out a harsh breath. "Now, let's try this again. Where the hell are you and who are you with?"

I make a tisking noise, similar to the one my mom used to make when I disappointed her, which happened a lot. "That is none of your damn business. I don't appreciate your attitude, so why don't you do us both a favor and leave me the hell alone. You're killing my buzz." I yell into the phone before disconnecting the call and throwing my phone back into my bag.

Glancing up, I notice Jane and Jax staring at me with wide eyes, their mouths hanging ajar. I absently wave my hand in their faces and laugh when neither of them blinks. They are in shock or something close to it.

When Jax goes to finally tries to say something, I speak up and cut him off. "Don't even say a word," I threaten, my finger wagging in his face like a sword. "Now, be a good friend and order me another drink before what I just did sinks in and I freak out."

With a concerned smile lighting her face, Jane slides her shot of tequila in front of me. I throw it back before I have a chance to change my mind. A beat later my phone begins singing again. The song "Crazy" is no longer an inside joke. Now it is a beat of doom similar to walking the plank or taking a drive off the top of a high building. Snatching it from my purse, I turn it off and bury it deep it in the bottom of my bag.

Out of sight, out of mind, right?

I clam up and listen to my friends retell their last week's events before taking up an old argument over which superhero would have a better chance of surviving an apocalypse. This conversation commenced close to three years ago and has gotten more elaborate over the years.

Jane's pick of superhero has morphed from Batman to Superman, and now the Hulk, unlike Jax, who has always stayed true to his choice of Spiderman. This is one of those arguments that never has an ending but always manages to get their tails ruffled. Tonight is no exception.

It doesn't take long before the tequila kicks in, and my vision takes a turn for the worse, going from slightly blurred to almost nonexistent. Everything around me is an odd mixture of shadows and distorted shapes, making my head pound and my eyes water. Jax moves to slide in next to me and with a sigh of defeat, I lay my heavy head against his shoulder, loving the way his soft shirt caresses my cheek.

"Do you want me to take you home, baby doll? That last shot was overkill, and I wouldn't be surprised if you end up sick. As much as I love you, I would rather not spend the rest of my night cleaning up your puke."

I grumble my displeasure at his teasing, but my protests turn to a purr as Jax strokes my hair. The small movement is comforting and quells my need to lash out at him.

"No, I'm fine," I mutter, burrowing my body further into his chest, which is too muscular to be considered comfortable. "Just let me lay my head here for a while."

I squeeze my eyes closed in hopes of stopping the room from spinning. It has been a long time since I drank this much, and even in my intoxicated state; I am dreading tomorrow and the hangover that is sure to come.

At some point, I must have fallen asleep, because when my eyes flutter open again, I am alone in the booth, curled up in a fetal position, with my hair draped across my face. I peel my cheek off the cheap vinyl seat, and wince as a stabbing sensation assaults my head, making it feel like a thousand knives are slashing through my muddled brain. The pain is all consuming, and it takes everything in me not to cry out.

I rub at my temples in hopes of alleviating some of the pressure while peering at the empty seats beside and in front of me with a raised brow. Where have my friends gone? *They better not have left me here.*

I slumped down in the seat and continued to rub my throbbing head when the sound of yelling blasts my ears, kicking my headache up another notch. My eyes flicker around the room seeking out the commotion as a sickly suspension takes root in the pit of my stomach. I try and push down my unease, but as the voices get louder and more heated. I can't deny the truth. I know those voices, as well as I know my own, but what I don't understand is why Alex and Jax are yelling at each other. Or why Alex is here.

Pulling myself out of the booth, I walk the short distance to where Jane is standing near the pool tables and lean against one as I take in the sight before me. I am finding it difficult not to stare at my two favorite men, currently standing toe to toe, each sporting their definition of a murderous glare.

I should be repulsed by their need to act stupid, but I'm not. Throw in some oil, fewer clothes, and some popcorn, and this could be a main event. It's like watching a messed up version of gladiators gone wild. Noticing my arrival, Jane's lips quirk up in a sympathetic smile.

"What the hell is going on?" I ask, apprehension making my voice sound small.

"Welcome back, Sleeping Beauty." She gives me a sad smile that makes my already queasy stomach even more upset.

"Where is Jax?" I ask.

"Right there," she says with a slight nod toward the current display of testosterone being played out before us. "You passed out after your phone call with Alex. Shutting off your phone was a bad move.

"Alex freaked out when he couldn't reach you. He found my number from our work contract and called, looking for you." She pauses and her expression turns somewhat guilty. "I did my best to reassure him you were fine. I told him we were out celebrating and blowing off some steam, but during our conversation, I got to talking too much. Without even meaning to, I slipped up and told him where we were."

I frown as her words sink in. "So, I guess Alex was not reassured?"

A giggle escapes her lips as her halo of blonde curls shake. "No, he was anything but reassured. Finding you passed out and laid out across Jax's lap only escalated matters. Heated words were exchanged, and then Alex demanded he take you home with him. Jax turned all big, protective brother and refused to release you.

"I about had a coronary when he told Alex to take a hike. This," she says pointing to both enraged men, "is the end result."

My face scrunches up as I contemplate how to handle this mess. I can't stand by and let Jax take the brunt of Alex's wrath. This is my problem, not his. In college, when a fight would break out at a party, a girl could pull her top up. A good show of breasts always ended a fight and got the guys to thinking about other things. I don't think that will work in this case.

"Okay," I say as I square up my shoulders. "I'm going to try and stop this. If I don't make it back out, know that you are a great friend. In the event of my demise, you are welcome to my collection of Julia Roberts movies and all the dark chocolate bars I've been hiding under the bread in the pantry. Wish me luck," I add for good measure.

"You sneaky bitch," she scoffs, her lips shaping into a pout. "I can't believe you've been hiding chocolate from me. I thought we were friends."

"Really?" I ask on an eye roll. "I'm about to throw myself into the lion's cage and face off with two irrational men, and that is your concern? You choose chocolate over my welfare?"

"You did say it was dark chocolate," she replies defensively. "Plus, if you went to the trouble to hide it, it has to be a good quality chocolate. Is bet it's Godiva or something equally yummy like Taza or Green and Black." Her enthusiasm for my chocolate is winning over her ability to stay in the here and now.

Ignoring my crazy friend, I step forward and position myself, so I am in between Alex and Jax. If either of them decide to attack the other, they will be taking me along for the ride. I can't stop a nervous smile from slipping to my face as both men fall silent, their full attention swinging straight to me.

I mentally slap myself for not coming up with a more solid plan. Anything has to be better than standing here like an idiot while praying they have a sudden change of heart and call a cease and desist. I am so tempted to lift my shirt up just for the hell of it. If their weighted expressions were not enough to make me second guess myself, Jane has to go and make it worse by humming the theme song to *Jaws* under her breath. I swear that girl is never getting her hands on my good chocolate after tonight.

Alex snares me with his gaze, drowning me in a sea of deep green. The raw emotion staring back at me steals my breath away. His eyes command my attention, and for the life of me, I can't force myself to look away. His eyes flicker over my body before traveling to my face once again, and it's that simple move that allows me to find my voice.

"Alex, I'm not sure why you are so upset, but if you want to be mad at someone, be mad at me, not my friends. They were doing as I asked. There is no way either of them would have let anything bad happen to me."

From the look on his face, you would have thought I had just told him I secretly had two heads and ate small children for breakfast. His expression quickly turns predatory, and suddenly, his mouth is on me, his lips smothering mine as his tongue strokes my own. My eyes close as the smell and heat of him wrap around me, easing my headache and making my body buzz from something much better than alcohol. Something that is becoming familiar and solely Alex.

My lips tickle as he speaks against them, his voice a smooth caress. "Get your stuff, Jessica. You're coming home with me for the night." His voice takes on a commanding edge that leaves no room for argument, so I don't.

Bewildered by the chain of events, I turn to thank Jax for stepping up and playing big brother for me. His hands wrap around my waist, yanking me into his chest and smothering me in a hug that is makes breathing a task.

With his body pinning me in place, I speak against his shirt, my voice coming out muffled and rough. "Thank you and please don't ever get that lovely face of yours rearranged on my account. I like it too much to see it hurt."

His deep laughs rumbled through me, making my lips tip up in a smile. "Anything for my girl."

I pulled back and stared up at him, my smile turning bigger by the second. "Anything?"

His eyes light up with humor as he flashes me a boyish grin. "Almost anything," he corrects. "If it involves protecting you, then yes, anything. But that does not mean I will let you dress me up in drag or make me cluck like a chicken in public for your and Jane's sick entertainment."

I snort, the thought of Jax in a dress making me cringe. "I'll keep that in mind."

Knowing that I am on borrowed time with Alex, I move back to the table and retrieve my purse.

Jane is quick to follow behind me. "Are you sure you want to go with him? You don't have to, Jess," she says, softly rubbing my back.

I shake my head. "I need to. I can't drink him away, so I might as well deal with him." Giving her a half smile, I kiss her on the cheek, and walk over and do the same to Jax.

"Thanks for looking after me, Jax. Sorry if I ruined your night."

"Baby doll, I would do anything for you," he says, lightly kissing the top of my head. "Are you sure you will be all right?"

"Yeah, I'm okay. Alex might act like a brute, but he's more growl than bite," I answer honestly. I don't know anything substantial about Alex, but I don't for one second believe that he is a closet serial killer. The only damage he can do is to my heart, and I don't plan on letting him get that close.

Before I can execute my escape, Jax leans down and whispers in my ear. "Turn your phone back on so we can reach you. Promise me you won't hesitate to call if you need anything."

Smiling at his handsome face, I open my mouth to tell him to stop worrying, but that thought is thrown out the window as I take in the concern staring back at me. Without objection, I pull my phone out of my bag and make a point of turning it on in front of him. Some of the tension etched on his face instantly leaves him.

Then, before I have a chance to say more, Alex moves in and pulls me against his side. With a pounding headache and troubled heart, I leave the bar.

Carson is once again standing beside the car, looking more like hired muscle than a chauffeur. Accepting his hand as he helps me into the backseat, I wait until he is back in behind the wheel, and the partition is up between us before I let my pent-up frustration lose on Alex.

"Why did you feel the need to harass my friends and me tonight? Jane already told you I was fine." My question comes out forceful, more so than I intended.

Alex is silent for a moment, his hand reaching up to shove a stray strand of hair from his eyes. My fingers twitch with a need to run my fingers through his hair, to touch him in some way, but I bolt down those feelings and keep them locked away where they belong.

He lets out a harsh sigh. "Don't ask stupid questions, Jessica."

The scowl on his face would typically make me bite my tongue, but my mouth is still running off the influence from my tequila earlier, and it knows no bounds. "You fucked me once," I say matter-of-factly. "That one act does not entitle you to play the hero card and come to my rescue. I have friends for that."

I can't help but swallow at the sudden intensity lurking behind his gaze. I try and control my breathing, but I found myself feeding off his wild emotions, and my rapid heart-beat kicked up another notch.

His hand lightly strokes my cheek, a sweet move that contradicts the turmoil beating within him. "Understand this, Jessica. I will always take care of those I care about. Hearing your voice on that phone and realizing you were intoxicated, upset, and not knowing who you were with or where you were shaved off ten years of my life. If you ever pull this shit again, I'll haul you over my knee and blister your stubborn ass until you can't walk straight."

I blink in surprise, biting down on my lip to keep the smile that is threatening to overtake me. Alex is worried. About me of all things. The great and powerful, Alex Harlow has a heart, and like the Grinch, the damn thing is growing.

I curl back in the soft, leather seats and stew on this new bit of information for the remainder of the drive. Once we arrive back at Glimmer, Carson is quick on his feet, kindly opening the door for me before I even have a chance to touch the handle. I follow Alex out of the car, knocking his hand away when he offers it to me and not because I am bitchy. I have a good reason.

He thinks I'm too drunk to stand on my own, and although he might be right, it still irritates me. Refusing to stumble and give him something else to complain about, I slip off my heels and tuck them under my arm, as I stomp toward the elevator with him following close behind.

The air in the elevator car is thick and filled with unspoken words as we ascend to the top floor. I fidget in place as his eyes bore holes in the back of my head. I refuse to turn around, afraid of what I might see, so instead I keep my eyes trained on the metal doors in front of me.

As the doors open, my feet kick into gear and take me straight through the entryway to the living room. I set my purse on an empty chair before shaking off my nerves and turning to face Alex as I finally muster up the courage to deal with him. I attempt a smile as my gaze sweeps over his features.

Absorbed in my fit earlier, I didn't take notice of his casual apparel. I've never seen Alex dressed down before, and I must say it suits him. Wearing a pair of loose, worn jeans that hug his hips like a lover and a black, ribbed T-shirt that outlines the definition in his upper muscles, he looks delectable and dangerous. I find my mouth shutting, and everything I had been about to say wiped from my mind.

Alex stands close enough that his signature scent of vanilla and cinnamon teases my senses. He moves with a purpose and brushes by me. I track his movements as he strides into the kitchen like a man on a mission. Curious as to what he is up to, I stand back and watch as him.

Retrieving a tall glass from one of the many cabinets, he fills it with water before going back to said cabinets and searching through each of them. He grumbles incoherent words as he moves from one to the other. It isn't long before he is back where I am standing, placing the glass of water in my hand along with two pain relievers.

"You will be dehydrated from all that liquor in your system. Drink all of the water with these." He points to the two little pills in my hand. "It will help to lessen the headache you will no doubt be feeling later," he says, his tone dry.

I sigh in defeat. Once again, he is back to being Mr. No Emotion. Licking my lips nervously, I try and think of what to say to break the tension growing between us, but find myself devoid of any words that might help. His stoic face is not giving anything away. I would welcome screaming and anger over this nothingness. Without giving me a second glance, he turns on his heel and heads down the hall toward his office. With a mighty slam, the door shuts soundly behind him.

I throw myself on the sofa and turn on the television. If he wants to be moody, then he can do it alone. I refuse to let his grumpiness rub off on me and ruin any more of my night. The movie *Friends with Benefits* is playing tonight. The longer I watch it, the more my focus drifts to other things. Important things.

For example, would my relationship with Alex be considered a friends with benefits type of thing? I don't think it would because we aren't friends. We aren't strangers either. So the question of the day is: *What the hell are we?*

We had sex only one time, and now Mr. Moody is calling me *his? What does being his entail?* Just one more question I will file away for a later date. Those damn unanswered questions are starting to add up.

Several hours and many infomercials later, Alex has yet to emerge from his office. I contemplate leaving and catching a cab home but dismiss the idea when I notice the time. Jane would kill me if I took a cab anywhere by myself at this hour. Rising from the couch, I walk to his bedroom and rifle through his drawers in search of something to sleep in.

Dressed in a pair of boxers and a T-shirt, I climb into his bed and tuck the sheets and comforter tightly around me so that when I am done I resemble a wrapped up tamale. His bed feels like what I imagine a cloud would. As comfortable as it is, I can't relax. I don't like being in here by myself while he stays in his office sulking away like a petulant child. What's worse is that I don't know why he's upset. His rapid mood swings confuse me like no other.

Why would he bring me here if he is going to ignore me? I feel like I'm being punished for something, but I don't know what I did to deserve the cold shoulder I'm getting. I toss and turn for a while mulling over everything before finally giving in and finding the sleep I so desperately need.

****

My body is on fire. A delicious, all-consuming heat spreads through my body, singeing everything in its path. My eyes flutter open. I blink away the haze of sleep as the room I'm in comes into focus. Confusion sets in as to why I'm awake. A memory of the bar, a ride Alex's limo, and those damn infomercials flutter through my mind before all the nights' events puzzle themselves out. Recognition hits me at the same time Alex's tongue skims over my wet core.

A small moan escapes my lips as my body roars to life under his skillful manipulation. His thumb lightly moves over my clit in a teasing manner as his index finger dips deep inside my pussy. My legs fall open, accepting his assault on my body and giving him full access to my dripping slit.

Alex's body shifts, so he is now laying in between my legs, his face mere inches from my sex. A part of me thinks I should be embarrassed at being this open to him, but I'm not. The intimacy of the situation is intense, and knowing that he can see how responsive I am to him turns me on further. I have had a few boyfriends who have gone down on me in the past, but none of them took the time to make it count. Hell, the majority of them never gave me an orgasm. They were all in a hurry to finish the deed at record-breaking speed so we could switch positions, and I would be the one giving them pleasure.

I squirm under his watchful gaze as he drives me to the brink of coming, only to stop and then start all over again. I wiggle my hips in an attempt to urge him on, but he just smiles and strengthens his hold on me. He is in control again and won't let me dictate when or how I will reach an orgasm. I'm putty in his hands as he torments me in the best way possible.

"I love how wet you get for me." He practically growls as his tongue swipes through my slippery folds, drinking in the wetness he has created.

I shiver from the contact. Alex continues to feast on my core, licking and tongue-fucking me until my sensitive flesh is so tender and swollen from his ministrations I am shaking beneath him. "Oh God!" I cry out. "Please, please, Alex...I am so close." I hate that he makes me beg, but in the state I am in, I can only do just that.

The sensations flowing through my body are so powerful they are almost painful. The throbbing in my core has built to a crescendo that is threatening to tear me in two. I'm shaking from the tip of my head to the heel of my foot as Alex slips in two more fingers. I squirm in a heated frenzy as my body soared higher. Alex works his finger in and out, adding a curling motion that throws me over the edge. I tried to swallow my moan, but it came out anyway. As if what I am experiencing isn't enough, Alex flicks his tongue over my hard clit and presses down on it firmly with the flat of his tongue.

"Fuck!" I scream as my body splinters into a million pieces. I gulp in large breaths of air as I attempt to slow my heart rate. It feels like my heart could beat out of my chest at any moment. I'm not sure if this is another orgasm ripping through me or just an encore from the first one. Either way, it blew my mind, turning all my inhibitions to dust.

"Give me your eyes, Jessica. I need to see your eyes as you come for me," he demands.

My eyes fly open and connect to his. His expression is fierce, possessive, and dangerously sexy. The desire is evident in his eyes, and I can only assume he sees the same thing in mine. As my orgasm waned, and my breathing returns to normal, he withdraws his fingers. Flashing me a wicked smile he brings his fingers up to my lips. "Lick me clean, baby. I want you to see how amazing you taste."

I stare at his fingers with apprehension. I've never tasted myself before. I meet his challenging gaze with my determined one. I'm learning that there is a pattern with Alex and his challenges. I think he gets off on bringing me out of my comfort zone. Pushing aside my fear, I tentatively stick my tongue out and taste my essence. Not turned off by the taste, I take his hand and bring each of his digits into my mouth, making a point to lick them all clean.

His eyes widen with surprise before turning hooded with lust. "That's my girl," he mutters, his voice sounding rough. "You are so damn beautiful."

Reaching down I grab the hem of his shirt that I am still wearing and pull it over my head before grasping his and repeating the motion. I want us to be skin on skin. I need to feel his naked flesh under my hands. Standing, Alex undoes his pants and pulls them off along with his boxers. As he climbs back down beside me, I take my time exploring every ripple and muscle on his chest.

Nipping and licking as I go, I memorize every inch and take note of the places that make him shudder. His nipples are extra sensitive. I get carried away with them, loving the way his chest heaves as I grate my teeth around them. Wrapping a hand in my hair, he gently pulls me up his body until we are once again face-to-face.

I capture his mouth with my own as my hands fist in his hair. I use the strands to anchor him to me as my mouth moves against his. The kiss is hot, wild, and all consuming. Our tongues battle and fight in an erotic dance that sends fire through my veins and has me wanting more. Desire hits me hard, pulsing through my body like a raging fire that refuses to be put out. Pulling away, he stares back at me. His gorgeous eyes are half-lidded and dark with passion.

"Are you ready for me, baby? Is your pussy ready for my hard cock?"

I bite my lip and try to hold back a moan as he grazes a hand over my breast. He rolls my pebbled nipple between his thumb and forefinger, and the primal noise I was so determined to keep to myself rolls out of my mouth along with several other incoherent sounds.

"Shut up and fuck me already," I bite back. My eyes roll back as I tremble under his touch, needing more, so much more.

I'm tired of playing games, and I'm ready to move on to the part where he is buried deep inside of me. Alex chuckles at my words. Instead of doing as I ask, he continues to play with my breasts, taking his time, and tormenting me to the brink of insanity. He palms each mound of flesh; my nipples pucker in response. Alex takes his time as he works me into a frenzy by pulling the tight buds into his hot mouth, sucking on them greedily, and lashing them with his talented tongue.

I pant loudly as my sex clenches with need. "Alex," I all but shout. "Stop being a cock tease!"

I'm on the cusp of exploding, but I don't want to fall over until he is buried deep within me. His hands tighten around my waist as he pulls me down, positioning me so that my slit is lined up with his hard erection. He fights to keep control, and all the while, I lay still, praying and hoping he loses the battle. I want to see him unravel and become the primal beast I see lying dormant under all those slick suits and polished manners.

Leaning back on his hunches, he takes hold of his thick cock and slides his hand up and down the shaft, while keeping his eyes trained on me. I lick my lips in anticipation. I've never craved someone as bad as this man. I groan as I feel the tip of his cock slide up and down my slit. I lose track of how long this goes on. He's teasing me, driving me mad with want as he shifts his cock head back and forth along my skin, coating himself in my juices. I try and push down on him, but he anticipates my moves and keeps himself at bay, never letting me take control and always making me plead for more. Which, of course, I do.

"Lift up your arms and grab hold of the top of the bed frame. Don't let go. If you do, I will stop whatever I'm doing." His tone leaves no room for questions.

Reaching above me, I do as I am told.

Alex's eyes darken with approval. "You are so beautiful laid out and open for me baby," he breathes.

Shifting his body, he grips my hips and with a forceful thrust, impales himself deep within my body. I cry out at the sudden intrusion while welcoming the sweet mixture of pain and pleasure that envelops me. His cock spreads me wide, the girth of it almost too much to handle. Alex braces himself above me and gives my body the time it needs to adjust to his size. Closing my eyes, I try and catch my breath.

"Christ, baby. You are unbelievably tight," he gasps. I arch up against him as his hips trust forward in precise movements, driving his cock deeper. "You feel amazing. Your warm pussy is wrapped around my cock like a vise," he murmurs, his breath warming my neck.

He grunts on every thrust, and I moan loudly in return. As he pulls me in close, I melt into him. I feel every inch of his body as it slides against me, hard and unyielding. I tilt up my hips and meet him thrust for thrust, loving the way his cock fills and stretches me.

A growl rumbled in the back of his throat. He pulls out and plunges back in, his movements rough and lacking the control he frequently exerts. "You feel incredible. We were made for each other. We belong together, baby."

I bite my lip and remain quiet. I'm scared to give him more power over me than he already has. I enjoy being around him, and the man can satisfy me like no one's business, but to say I belong to someone goes beyond the bedroom, and I'm not ready for that. At least, I don't think I am. Hell, I have no idea what I'm ready for anymore. He's got my emotions all twisted up and turned around.

Knowing my game and not one to go down without a fight, Alex's eyes narrow and take on a challenge I never meant to throw down. To my surprise, he seats his cock deep in my center and stills his hips. The pressure of having him fill me completely and yet not moving is unbearably cruel. I buck against him and try to coax him to answer my plea, but it's no use. He won't move an inch.

"You're punishing me," I accuse. Moisture burns my eyes as my frustration mounts. "This isn't fair, Alex. You can't make me trust you enough to give myself over freely. Relationships doesn't work that way."

Reaching for my breast, he rubs my taut nipple between his fingers, making my body ache for more. For him. I feel mindless and needy as I grind my hips, trying to get the friction I need to come. Alex chuckles and clamps down on my hips rendering my movements senseless as he plays with me.

He slowly rocks his cock in me once, twice and then stops all movement once more. Pulling away from my touch, he waits me out. "Say the words, Jessica. I want to hear you beg for me."

I groan, frustrated and beyond caring anymore. I can't resist him. As if knowing this, Alex ups the ante by reaching a hand between us to rub his thumb in small circles over my sensitive clit. His skilled fingers are my undoing.

I cry out, begging Alex for release. I would promise him the world right now if he let me come. "I'm yours, Alex. All yours." My voice cracks as I continue to yell. I grip the headboard with all my might as my body trembles with need. "Now please shut up and fuck me. I want you."

With a triumphant smile, he hammers into me, the thrusts delectable and strong. It doesn't take long before I'm back on the cusp of a heady orgasm, one that will no doubt have me seeing stars. He kisses me. Our tongues tangle together, sampling each other and riding out the pleasure our bodies create.

His pelvis rubs my core in a delicious rhythm that sends me over the edge. I detonate; my screams resonate through the air as the world shatters around me. My whole body trembles and shakes as my walls suck and pull him in deeper. Alex grunts and growls as he continues to thrust his hips fast and hard, his control unraveling as his movements become erratic and wild. With a loud yell, his cock pulses within me. His body goes stiff as he holds onto me tightly.

His voice repeatedly murmurs my name while his cock jerks inside of me, bathing my insides with his cum.

I let out a laugh, surprised by the turn of events. If someone had told me that within twenty-four hours, I would go from wanting to shove my foot up Alex's ass to screaming out his name like a prayer to God above, I would have called them a liar. How can one man make me madder than hell and then in a blink of the eye, have me smiling larger than life itself? *It's so messed up and twisted.*

With both of us spent and tired. Alex collapses behind me as we lay cuddled with my back to his chest, and our legs entwined. The silence between us is pleasant and soothing. I'm just about asleep again when he jolts behind me, effectively ruining my post-coitus bliss.

"Shit to all hell." Alex hisses through clenched teeth. Pushing me aside as if his ass were on fire, he jumps out of bed with a look of pure panic written across his face. "Why the hell didn't you warn me?"

I sit up in bed and rub at my eyes, confused as to what he is going on about. I am not the least bit pleased with his accusing tone. "What is your problem?"

"I didn't wear a condom." He runs a hand through his disheveled hair as he paces the floor. "I never forget to wear a condom."

"Oh." I blush, embarrassed for being so careless, not to mention stupid. I am normally a saint when it comes to making sure a guy wraps it up before sex. This just proves that whenever I am near Alex my brain goes on a hiatus.

"Are you on the pill?" He glances my way, his face looking grim. Talk about a mood killer. Nothing like the chance of catching an STD or an unplanned pregnancy to ruin a perfectly good cuddling session.

I nod my head. "Yeah, I've been on birth control for several years now. I'm also clean and get tested regularly. What about you?"

A look of relief spreads across his face and his eyes soften. "I'm clean, baby. I'm sorry for before. I shouldn't have entered you bare without speaking to you about it first. I wasn't thinking.

Alex smiles briefly. Taking my hand in his he kisses my fingers tips. "I would prefer not wearing a condom with you in the future. Being inside you bare was fucking unbelievable. I don't want anything between us ever again. Is that okay with you?"

I'm torn on how to respond. I have never purposely been with a guy without a condom before. Not even Travis got that privilege, and I had planned on marrying that jerk. Do I trust him enough to allow this?

Yes.

Do I think he could hurt me if this ever turns into something more serious?

Yes.

Even with the odds not in my favor, I have a hard time saying no to him. Especially, when he gives me that wolfish smile he keeps shooting my way. "We've already taken the plunge, even if it was a mistake. So yeah, that's fine with me."

He smiles like a kid who just experienced his first Christmas. I mean, a full-blown, teeth-showing smile that I've never seen before. I am so used to seeing him frown, I am shocked by what a great smile he has. *He should do that more often.*

Grabbing my hand, he pulls me out of bed, and with my hand in his, he leads me across the room to his bathroom. "Let's shower, and then I will get you some breakfast."

Walking a step or two behind him, I stare at his backside and enjoy the view. I've never been much of ass person, but Alex's ass is perfectly round, taut and dare I say...sexy. The damn thing begs to be fantasized about. I plop down on top of the vanity while he gets the shower water the right temperature.

I'm confused by my warped feelings and need to be with a man like Alex. He is everything I've been trying to stay away from, and yet, here I am, bumping uglies with him and wanting more.

What's a girl to do?

Attempting to ignore him doesn't work. In fact, that only seems to drive him to try harder. We could spend the rest of our lives in his bed getting it on, and it would still not be enough to wipe him from my system. My need to be with him is stronger than ever. *Can I be with him and keep my heart out of this?* That is the million-dollar question.

Feeling Alex's gaze burning a hole through me, I jump off the counter before he has a chance to question what's on my mind. Wrapping an arm around my waist, he pulls me against him and under the spray of the warm water. My skin is flushed and heated, and it has nothing to do with the water temperature.

With my back nestled against his chest, he reaches around and grabs the bar of soap from the carrier built into the tile. Lathering up his hands, he rubs the soap across my shoulders in a kneading, circular motion, before moving down to my arms, stomach, and finally to my breasts. I lean my head back on his shoulder and let out a small groan as my body relaxes and gives in to his ministrations. I have never had a man take the time to wash me before. The whole experience is incredibly erotic and sexy. I think this is my new favorite thing.

"I love the way your body responds to my touch," he murmurs as his fingers circle my taut nipple causing sparks to race up my spine.

"Hmmm." I respond. Not the best response I've ever had, but with my mind turning into mush that is the only answer I can come up with at the moment. Despite what you may hear, being horny and witty at the same time is a feat very few can pull off. I apparently don't have that skill.

His hand trails down my stomach and briefly plays with my belly button before slipping his fingers between my thighs and through my wet folds. He pulls me back into his arms, and I gasp as his growing erection is pressed into my lower back.

His skillful fingers work my body like a pro as his lips continue to lick and tease my neck with soft kisses. I squirm in his arms as the heel of his hand grinds against my clit while two fingers are pumping roughly in and out of my slick channel.

"Oh shit," I cry as his fingers zones in on my G-spot, stroking it with the right amount of pressure. Closing my eyes, I let the sensations take me over as I boldly ride his hand, rocking my hips as I take what I need.

"Come for me, baby," Alex softly commands, and like a puppet on stupid string, my body responds and answers his call. With a jerk, I dive over the edge of bliss. My legs threaten to give out as my pussy quivers, clamping down on his fingers and milking them as he continues to torment my hyper-sensitive clit. It's all too much. With a steel grip on my hips, Alex holds me up as my orgasm continues to wash over me, stealing me of breath and robbing me of my senses.

Wrapped up in his arms, he continues to watch over me and keeps the spray of water off my face while I bask in my post-orgasmic haze.

"That was...wow." Once again, wittiness fails me, leaving me to search for words that elude me. I blink my eyes back into focus. Dipping my head back, I allow the onset of water to pour over my head, praying that it will help in cooling off my flushed cheeks.

"I aim to please, Ms. Grayson," Alex grabs the bar of soap and places it in my hands. "Turn around and face me. It's your turn to clean me."

I laugh as I lather the soap into suds. "I don't think there's enough soap in the world to make you clean and pure, Mr. Harlow." He snorts at my comment, and I silently pat myself on the back for finally getting some of my sass back.

Turning to face him, I place my soapy hands on his chest and make slow circles across his pecs, taking my time to enjoy the show of muscles before me. I follow the same path he took with me down his chest, and by the time I reach his cock, he is rock hard and ready for me. Just the way I like him.

Glancing up at his face, I give him a seductive grin as I take my time crawling down his body before sinking to my knees in front of him. Ignoring the hard tiles digging into my knees, I wiggle around to adjust my position and marvel at the glorious cock standing at attention before me. I don't usually think of a man's erection as beautiful, but his is. Alex's package is the perfect mixture of length and girth needed to make a girl spread her legs and beg for more.

Licking my lips, I reach forward and grip his length firmly in my hands. Sticking my tongue out, I swipe it against the rigid crown, lapping up the beads of moisture that had seeped out.

"Jessica," he groans. "You killing me. Take me in that pretty mouth of yours, love. I want you to fuck me with your mouth."

I blink and give him a nod. With one hand massaging his balls and the other stroking up and down the base of his length, I place the crown of his cock against my lips and take him in my mouth as deep as possible without activating my gag reflex. His fingers thread through my hair and with a gentle tug, Alex guides my movements.

His heated gaze scorches me. "You look gorgeous in that position. There is nothing sexier than seeing a beautiful woman, naked, on her knees, and ready to pleasure me."

Feeling a bit more confident, I take more of him into my mouth and swirl my tongue around his cock, loving the taste and texture of him on my tongue. Alex leans his head back on the tile and closes his eyes. With an unhappy growl, I make a point to chastise him, the same way he always does me. "Eyes on me, Alex. I want to see those gorgeous, emerald globes of yours."

He chuckles. I use my tongue and hands to explore him thoroughly. It doesn't take long for me to find a good rhythm. Paying attention to his facial expressions, I gage what he likes and what seems to drive him wild. Raking my teeth around the sensitive tip, he groans loudly and raises his hips, pushing more of himself into my mouth until he bumps the back of my throat.

"Damn, baby, your mouth feels like heaven," he rasps through clenched teeth. His face is drawn up tight, and I can tell he is fighting hard to hold himself together. I don't want him in control. I want him wild and uninhibited. The water rains down my back and I move my hands up to Alex's hips for support. My need for him becomes aggressive. Hollowing my cheeks, I suck him deeper and harder, giving him the best, deep-throat experience he's ever had. At least that is what I am aiming for.

With a tug of my hair, Alex commands my eyes to seek him out, and they do. "I'm ready, baby. If you don't want me to cum in that luscious mouth of yours, then you need to stop right now." His raspy voice sends small tremors through me.

There is no way I'm going to stop. Watching Alex fall apart under my touch is the closest I've ever come to nirvana. Gripping his hips tighter, I keep him seated in my mouth while I suck him faster and harder. Screaming out a strangled groan, Alex thrusts his hips once more against my face, and his cock throbs in my mouth right before spurts of his salty cream slips down my throat.

My pussy drips with want as I lick away the last drops of his essence. I never thought giving a blowjob could be such a turn on. It's definitely a first for me. Alex pulls his cock from my mouth and slumps against the back shower wall, his breathing ragged and heavy, despite the sated smile gracing his face. I stand up with a triumphant grin. *I feel like doing a happy dance.* I turned the glorious Alex Harlow to putty in my hands!

Reaching for my hand, he brings it to his mouth and plants a sweet kiss on the center of my palm. "That was amazing." The gesture was unexpected and hit me straight between the legs. My brows rise as I take in this new side of him. I can't help but wonder how much of it is for real and how much is for show.

"You are amazing."

The admission stuns and confuses me once again. "Thank you." My cheeks heat as I blush like a stupid schoolgirl. It's absurd to become shy after everything we've done, but our level of intimacy keeps climbing at record-breaking speed, throwing me into uncharted territory.

Alex turns off the water and steps out of the shower, pulling me with him. Drying off, he wraps a towel around his waist before holding out a large white fluffy towel for me to do the same.

Without a word, I follow suit. As I move around the bathroom, his eyes follow my progress. Wrapping the towel around my body, I suddenly realize I have no clean clothes or toiletries with me. I curse under my breath as I comb the tangles from my hair with my fingers. Retreating to the bedroom, I go in search for the one thing I did bring with me, my purse.

I'm on the urge of freaking out. I can't find my purse any-where. I looked in all the normal places like the living, bed-room, and kitchen and even several unusual hiding spots like under the bed, in the closet and the kitchen pantry. I'm trying not to panic, but I can feel it mounting with each minute that ticks by.

"Babe, what in the hell are you doing?" Alex asks when he finds me sprawled on the floor with my ass up in the air as I search under the kitchen table for the second time.

I blow out a heavy breath of air. "I can't find my purse. I'm trying to use one of Jane's tricks and retrace my steps."

"Oh. I think I remember seeing it in the living room. Have you tried there yet?"

I tilt my head up and give him my best you're-an-idiot look. "Of course I have. You think this was the first place I chose to look? Good grief," I spout off, as I crawl back out from under the table.

Re-tying the towel around my body, I stomp past him toward the living room so I can prove to Mr. Know-It-All that he is wrong. I am in no way going crazy. I make two trips around the couches with Alex's help before we find my purse tucked up under a pillow on one of the recliners. Despite being happy to have found it, I am pissed that he was right. I know I looked in here before.

Ignoring Alex's soft chuckles, I retrieve my phone out of the side pocket of my purse and send a text to Jane letting her know that I'm doing well and plan on coming home later in the day. We typically spend our Saturday mornings cleaning the apartment together and getting up-to-date on our laundry. I like to think of myself as an equal opportunity roommate, meaning I would never ask her to clean up our mess alone.

Scrolling through my phone, I'm surprised to find that I've missed two text messages from Jane, one from Jax, and three missed calls from a private caller. The text messages from my besties are them just checking in on me. I study the message saying "Private Caller" with furrowed brows.

I don't ever get calls from private numbers. Jane and I listed my phone as the emergency, after-hours number for work. I make a point to keep all of our current and previous clients listed in the profile database for this reason. If any of them call me, it will show up on the screen by their name, not as "Private Caller." With a touch of a button, I check the details on the calls and find that they all came in between one and four o'clock this morning.

Lost in thought, I jump, surprised when Alex comes up behind me and wraps his arms around my waist. Placing two fingers under my chin, he tilts my head to the side and gives me a chaste kiss on my forehead. "You look perplexed. What's got you bothered?" Alex asks, his narrowed eyes punching holes through me.

I smile despite myself. "Nothing. I was just checking my phone and sending a text to Jane. Looks like I missed some messages from her and Jax last night." I ignore his questioning look and continue. "I think they were both afraid you might lock me in your secret dungeon and throw away the key."

Alex chuckles, and I sink into him as his chest vibrates against my back. "You'll always be safe with me. Plus, being the gentleman I am, I've already spoken to your friend Jane."

I feel him smile against the nape of my neck. "You did?" I ask clearly surprised.

"Yeah. We talked early this morning after she called my phone. I assured her you were in good hands and not shackled to my bed, drugged, or harmed in any way." He laughs. "She is a persistent little thing." Spinning me around in his arms, he sets his steely eyes on me. "Is that the only reason you're unnerved?"

Am I that transparent? I shrug and throw my phone back into my purse. "I've missed several calls from a private number. I find it odd. I'm sure I am blowing the whole thing out of proportion. It was probably just a wrong number."

Alex's lips press together in a hard line. I cringe, wondering if he is going to push me for answers I don't have, but to my delight he changes the subject. "I'm starved. Let's go cook breakfast," he says, smacking my ass on his way to the kitchen. "Why don't you go throw on some of my clothes until yours arrive."

My mouth opens and closes a few times. *Huh?* "What are you talking about?"

"I sent Carson out on your behalf. He is buying some clothes for you while your other ones are being cleaned. What you had from last night were wrinkled and reeked of smoke from that bar I found you in." His nose scrunches as he says it, apparently still sore about having to track me down and finding me inebriated. "I thought you would enjoy something clean to wear."

I let out a long breath as I flick him an irritated look. I'm not sure how I feel about him buying clothes for me. Or Carson picking them out. The more I try and puzzle out my feelings the irater I become. *God, I hope Carson he has good taste.*

"Seriously?" I blurt out, throwing my hands on my hips for good measure. "Why would you send Carson to buy me clothes? That is a bit extreme, Alex. Even for you. I don't need you to buy me clothes, let alone sending one of your employees running out and fetching them."

An emotion runs over his features, too fast for me to read, and then his jaw tightens up and his shoulders square. "You needed something to wear. I handled it. Although I love seeing you parade around in my clothes, they practically fall off you. There is no way in hell I am letting you go out in public half-clothed."

I stare at his back, seething, while he spends his time in the kitchen gathering up ingredients to make us breakfast, oblivious to the daggers I am shooting his way. If looks could kill, Alex would be pushing up daisies. "You're wrong," I argue, finally finding my voice.

I shoot him an exasperated look; one he finally notices. Ordering people around and making choices for others might be how things are done in his world, but that is not how things are done in mine. "I appreciate the thought, but next time ask me before deciding for me. I don't like you making decisions on my behalf."

His hands halt on mixing the eggs. Bracing his arms on the counter, he grips the cold granite and drops his head to his chest. I strain to listen, swearing that I can faintly hear him counting backward.

"Fine," he grits through clenched teeth. "I will take the time and confer with you next time. But understand that if I believe my way is more practical, your opinion will be overruled." Letting out a sound a lot like a growl, he releases the counter top and goes back to cooking breakfast.

I'm not happy. Not by a long shot, but I also know how to pick my battles, and I am smart enough to know I don't stand a chance against him on this. At least not today. Holding the towel tighter to my chest, I stomp back into the bedroom in search of something to put on. I dress quickly in another pair of his boxers and a t-shirt.

I pause before heading back to the kitchen to rejoin Alex. I'm still too riled up to face him and play nice, so instead I take a detour and check out his room further. With the scent of aftershave and cinnamon, there is no mistaking that this is Alex's room. It smells just like him. Glancing around, my eyes zone in on the framed photos decorating his walls. I frown, not knowing how I missed these before.

Clustered in a group on the far wall are several photos of what appear to be of his parents and what I assume are his grandparents, aunts, and uncles. The family resemblance between him and his dad is remarkable. As I study the picture closer, I pick out the similarities between the two of them such as a strong jaw, straight nose structure, and distinct broad shoulders. With a large smile on his face, the Alex in these pictures looks nothing like the serious man who keeps me on my toes and has turned my life into three-ring circus.

Moving onto another set of family photos, I screech to a halt when I find a new face standing in the midst of the others. My brows pinch together as I scan the picture. Perched beside Alex is a stunning girl close to my age. She has long, straight, blonde hair, striking blue eyes, and with her eyes locked on him, she has a wistful expression on her face. She looks nothing like the rest of his family, and yet she is posing with them and looking at Alex in an intimate way that unnerves me. I tap the photo with my finger wishing it could speak to me and answer the questions swirling in my head. *Who is she?* Before my mind can unravel who the mystery girl is, I hear Alex calling my name.

Walking out, I am pleasantly surprised to find Carson standing by the doorway. "I hope you find everything in here to your liking," he says, holding out a large white bag. I smile and thank him for his thoughtfulness. With a small wave, I hurry back to the bathroom to get dressed and fix my hair before it dries and turns into a giant clump of tangles that no amount of brushing can undo.

My initial worry was unwarranted. Carson is a natural shopper with a keen eye for style. Digging into the bag like a kid on Christmas day, I find a handful of designer jeans and matching tops ranging from silk to the softest cotton. Lining the bottom of the bag is a stash of sexy lace panties and delicate bras along with an assortment of makeup and hair products. Checking the tags, I get weirded out when I notice that everything in my size - and I mean everything - as in my underwear and bras also.

Either someone is a closet psychic or Alex has been snooping in my things, putting his nose where it does not belong. Both options upset me to the point where I refuse to leave my personals unattended around him anymore. My face heats to an unbearable level when I think of Carson picking out my unmentionables. *Very creepy!*

I dress quickly and throw my hair up in a high pony-tail that sways with my every step. Following the scent of bacon and something sweet, I make my way back to the kitchen just as Alex is laying the last serving plate on the table. As if on cue, my stomach growls its approval at the spread in front of me. I blink in surprise at the array of bacon, eggs, toast, strawberries with cream, and my all-time favorite, chocolate chip waffles, are laid out in front of me. I don't know how he does it. First, the correct size in my clothes and now all my favorite foods. There is no way that this can be a coincidence.

Someone is being stalkerish again. *My narrowed eyes zoom in on him.*

"Don't give me that look," he warns, a bit of humor laced in his voice. "Jane was a lot of help. When I spoke to her earlier, she gave me some pointers on your favorite things and what you might need to get ready."

My brows knit together as I absorb that bit of infor-mation. I'm surprised Jane trusted him enough to give him pointers. I cock my head to the side as my eyes take him in. "Checking up on me again, Mr. Harlow?"

"Just doing a little research on my favorite subject, Ms. Grayson."

I bite back a smile and turn my attention back to the food set before me. Without needing to be told, I dig in. Everything tastes amazing. I don't know many men who could have pulled this off by themselves. I'm impressed, not that I will be letting him know that. Lord knows, the man's head is large enough, no reason to go and make it any bigger. I had filled my plate with a little of everything and after eating more than I intended, I push back my plate and give my thanks to the chef. "That was good, Alex. What other talents are you hiding from me?"

A wry smile appears on his lips. "Keep looking at me like that and I'll carry you back to my bedroom and spend the day giving you a personal demonstration of all my many talents."

My heart flutters wildly in my chest, and I fight the urge to scream yes. Images of us tangled together run rampant through my mind. Thinking about all the delicious things he could do to my body has my mind stuck in dirty town with no hope of coming home any time soon.

My mind rushes back to the here and now when Alex clears his throat. Seeing the tension in his stance and the lines of worry etched on his face, my palms begin to sweat. I don't know what is going on, but it doesn't take a genius to figure out that something bad is on the horizon. I've seen Alex confident, arrogant, angry, sexy, and several other descriptive adjectives, but I have never seen him nervous. I chew on my lip, as I mentally prepare myself for the worst.

Alex approaches me with his arms folded across his chest. I mimic the movement and give him my best spit-it-out-already look. After what feels like forever, he finally speaks. "When you finish getting ready, we need to head into the city and find you a formal dress. I'm not picky on the color as long as it is something sleek, sexy, and preferably short."

"Alex..." I stop and give myself a chance to catch my breath before I lose my shit and end up screaming out obscenities I might later regret. Everyone has their limit and I have no doubt I've met mine. Once I feel a little calmer, I try again. "Alex, why do I need a formal dress?"

"For Tuesday night. I have a charity event I have to attend. It's something I go to every year. You'll be my plus one. As my date, of course," he adds, as if I couldn't figure that one out on my own.

I give my head a shake. I'm growing sick and tired of being told what to do. "No, I'm not," I snap back, not taking a moment to consider my answer. My blood begins to boil as my temper rises. I'm mad. No, correct that, I am furious with him. How dare he think he can make decisions for me without even taking the time to ask me?

Alex shoots me an exasperated look, and it takes everything in me not to stick my tongue out at him. I know it's childish, but what can I say, he brings out the best in me.

His tone changes to one of annoyance. "I swear you are the most difficult female I have ever met, and considering how many women I've known, that is saying a lot. Before you discount my invitation so harshly at least hear me out first."

Still unsure of what is happening between us and where we stood with each other, I hesitate. Drumming my fingers on the table, my eyes track his movements, taking in his tense body language and clenched jaws. Hoping to avoid a few rounds of fighting this early in the day, I manage a small nod. "Fine," I huff, sitting back in my chair. "Unlike you, I can play fair. Now, please, do tell me why I should be your date to this event? An event you conveniently forgot to mention anything about until now."

His body visibility relaxes as he chooses to not pick up on my flabbergasted tone. I doubt Alex is used to hearing the word "no." Well, if he plans on hanging out with me beyond today, then he better get used to hearing it more often.

"It's a charity event." He settles his hand on top of mine. The need to pull my hand back is high, but I put on my big girl panties, grit my teeth, and leave it alone. "It's held once a year and includes the crème of the crop of Dallas's top business moguls.

"Some of them, I would consider friends. The rest are tools who lucked out in the gene pool and were born with a never-ending trust fund and a solid-gold rattle. Being my date to this event would be a smart business move on your part. I can guarantee that you will meet influential people there who could help in building up your business portfolio. Meeting them would be a step in the right direction for you and Jane."

Words fail me. Instead of speaking, I sit there like a statue and stare at his mouth as it moves while taking it all in. I hate to admit it, but the bastard has a good point. The charity event would be an enormous opportunity for Jane and me.

I hesitate to answer, but it is pointless. It would be professional suicide to turn down his offer, and yet, the childish side of me refuses to give in so easily. Something about making Alex sweat out my answer has me doing a happy dance inside. So, instead of agreeing right away, I shrug my shoulders and say, "I'll think it over."

"I don't have all day for you to think it over," he chides. His voice sounds upset despite the blank expression on his face.

I smile in return.

"I don't understand," he muses, running a hand through his already disheveled hair. "Why did you turn me down right away?" His jaw is tight and his eyes narrowed.

He might act as though my answer has the power to hurt him, but I know better. What we have is fun and intense, but what he refuses to acknowledge is that it is fleeting. It might take a week or even a month, but Alex will lose interest in me once he feels I am no longer a challenge. Guys like him are always looking for the next best thing and my time is already a ticking.

Swallowing hard, I give him an honest answer. "I have accepted that running from you is a losing battle, but that does not mean I have any intention of doodling your name on my notebook like some love-sick teenager. We have great chemistry. You can hold a decent conversation when you're not all possessive and caveman-like, and you fulfill all my check marks in the bedroom. But I'm not delusional enough to pretend that we are both in this for the long haul. I'm okay with that fact, and you should be too. "

His head cocks to the side, and Alex stares at me for what feels like an eternity. His voice is soft when he speaks. "Who broke you, Jessica?"

I shake my head slowly and take a shuddering breath. Every intake of air hurts. My lungs feel constricted, as if there is a band around them and with each second that ticks by, it tightens a little bit more. My eyes dart around the room, landing on anything and everything, but him. His words have hit too close to home, and I don't like it. Out of desperation, I do the only thing I know to do. I feign ignorance.

I pull my hand from his and give him a pleading look. Pleading for what, I'm not sure. "You're acting crazy, Alex. No one broke me. I'm fine. Do us both a favor and stop trying to figure me out or *this*," I say, pointing a finger between the two of us, "will end right now." I try and keep my voice strong, but it cracks in the end.

Alex stands and turns away for a moment as if considering my words. If it weren't for his tense jaw and steely eyes, he would almost look relaxed. Almost, but not quite. His calm demeanor is nothing but a facade. Like always, his mind is busy at work, trying to find ways to make my walls come tumbling down. All I can say to that is game on.

"I will drop it for now, but only because we have a big day ahead of us. Trust me when I say that this conversation is far from finished." Reaching for my hand, he hauls me up and into his arms while holding me solidly against his body. Pressing a possessive kiss on my lips, he milks away all the stress of the morning, while making me forget that I'm supposed to be upset with him. *Clever bastard.*

He presses into me, and my body trembles with need. Pressing his face into the crook of my neck he whispers against my skin. "Let's go find you a dress, my beautiful girl."

Chapter Nine

"Jessica!" Jane yells. "Don't you dare fall asleep on me. There will be no sleeping until this movie is over. I have to know how it will end, or I won't be able to sleep tonight." I duck just in time to miss a throw pillow that goes sailing by my head.

"I'm wasn't trying to sleep," I lie. I will never understand why Jane chose to watch *The Thing* tonight. Scary movies and Jane do not mix. Two months ago, I had to put my foot down and stop her from watching the television series *The Walking Dead* after *the incident*.

That is what we are calling Jane's spur of the moment shopping spree at the local sporting store where she loaded up on baseball bats, shovels, and enough camouflage equipment to supply a small army. All of those things now reside in our spare closet in preparation for the day when zombies decide to take over the world.

As another pillow comes flying my way, I throw up my hands in surrender. "Why must you always torture us both by watching movies that bother you so much? Maybe you should stick to romance, comedies, and your local PBS station," I tease. A chuckle escapes my lips before I can clamp down on it.

"When is that fancy party you and Alex are going to?"

I roll my eyes at her obvious chance of subject. "It's a charity event, not a party, and it's this coming Tuesday," I huff, not wanting to discuss my upcoming date. "Just thinking about it gives me hives. I'm so afraid I am going to make a fool out myself," I admit, my body cringing from the thought. "I looked the event up on the web and the attendance list is freaking unbelievable. Every large, local magazine will be there along with some celebrities who work within our profession. If I can get even half of them to talk to us, we will be set with steady work for at least the next five years."

"I totally agree. I've got to be honest." She gives me a pointed look. "If you had turned him down, I would have been upset with you. I understand your reasons for wanting to protect yourself from getting in too deep with him, but you can't turn down a once in the lifetime opportunity because you fear commitment."

"Only you would try pimping me out for business connections," I counter with a laugh. "What's next? How about offering a blowjob for all renewing clients?"

Between hiding her face in a pillow and trying to watch the movie, she shoots me the middle finger. I would return the message, but she is once again engrossed in the movie and is no longer paying me a bit of attention.

I clear my throat until she finally looks over at me. "Seriously though, do you like my dress? I'm nervous about it being too much?"

"Hell, no. I love your dress. It is beyond beautiful, and you will look fabulous in it. I know I am supposed to be anti-Alex, but that was very sweet of him to buy you a designer dress like that and all accessories to match. My man would never think of going out of his way like that." Ignoring my snort of disbelief, she gets up and heads to the kitchen to refill her drink.

"I would have been happier about it all if he had let me pay for it. I hate feeling as if I owe anyone anything," I say, somewhat disappointed.

"Oh, please," she barks out with a snort. "You don't owe him diddly squat. He invited you, not the other way around, so if anything, you are doing him a favor. Plus, the man is loaded. It would take more than a measly designer dress and pair of high-dollar shoes to put a dent in his checkbook."

The sound of my phone singing the song "Crazy" brings our conversation to a halt. Her eyes widen as she glances at each. "That's just creepy." She laughs. "If I didn't know better, I would think he knows that we were talking about him."

I blanch at her words, not putting anything past him. In fact, breaking into my home and adding cameras and wires sounds like child's play for him. The man was like a bloodhound when it came to snooping and searching out information he required. For whatever reason, I've become his latest target. *Yeah, me!*

I pick up my phone. "Hi, Alex," I answer on a sigh.

"Hey, sweetheart. Have you changed your mind yet?" I smiled despite my internal nerves. Hearing his gravelly voice sends my hormones into overdrive. Which is exactly why I had told him no earlier when he asked me to come over.

"Sorry Alex, but my mind is made up. One night of sleeping by yourself in that all-too-comfy, large bed of yours won't kill you. You had me to yourself all day yesterday, and you'll be seeing me again in two days for the charity event."

Declining his offer earlier wasn't easy, but needed. I don't want to turn into one of those clingy girls I always pity. A little breathing room to clear my head is never a bad thing. Plus, I've missed Jane. Once again, Alex isn't handling being rejected with grace. I've lost count to how many times he's called trying to change my mind. His attempt at bribing me with chocolate and sex was a new low. As tempting as a chocolate-covered penis sounds, I held my own and didn't give in.

Instead, I spent the day with Jane cleaning the apartment, buying groceries, and getting all of our laundry cleaned and sorted. She's been missing David something awful. To cheer her up, I promised her tonight would be a girl's only night. She got to pick out the movie, and I ordered the pizza. Hence the reason we are watching *The Thing* and not something funny and uplifting like *Runaway Bride.*

"That does not work for me, Jessica," he answers, sounding tired. "I miss you and would prefer spending the night with you."

"Just sleep?"

His laugh is rich and full, sending tremors up and down my spine. "We can sleep. After my cock has worked over your dripping cunt and your voice is gone from shouting my name, I am sure you will need a few hours of sleep," he adds with a sexy groan.

My clit throbs with his every dirty word, making me wet and needy. I open my mouth to speak but close it, not trusting my voice not to give me away. I hate the emotions he pulls out of me, but at the same time, I love the way he makes me feel. When I am with him, I feel alive. It's scary and thrilling all at once.

When I refuse to answer, he does something I should have expected, and yet it still takes me by surprise. "If you won't come to me, then I am coming to you."

What? Oh hell no.

"Alex, that's not happening." My stupid heart tries to leap from my chest at the chance to see him despite my words conveying the opposite. "Stay home. I promised Jane a girl's only night, and that significant thing hanging between your legs disqualifies you from joining us."

"See you in twenty minutes." Before I can argue or threaten him with bodily harm, the line goes dead.

I stare down at the phone in disbelief. He hung up on me. *The controlling bastard hung up on me.* I glance over at Jane to find her with a big smile on her face, clearly delighted with my predicament. At least one of us is enjoying themselves.

I lean back in the couch and fill my cheeks with air before blowing it out slowly. I'm not used to feeling defeated, and it's not setting well with me. "He says he is on his way over. He hung up before I could say talk him out of it. Do you mind?" I am unsure of whether she will be okay with this or want to throttle me. "I have no problem kicking him out if you want to keep it strictly a girl-power night. He deserves being shut out."

Jane made a face. "I don't care. I find the whole back and forth banter between you two amusing. You've met your match with him. I never thought I would ever meet anyone as stubborn as you are. It's poetic justice," she says with a laugh.

"You're delusional," I counter with a very unladylike snort. "I'm a novelty to him. He isn't the type to continue seeing me for longer than is necessary. Surely you've read

all those articles about him in the magazines. He's a playboy. I'll play along and enjoy the ride while it lasts, but in
the end he'll grow tired of me just like he has with all the
others."

"Why do you always have to be such a downer?"

I duck as another round of pillows come flying my way.
Scooping them up before she can reclaim them, I tuck them
behind my back and give her a one finger salute.

"You're no fun," she pouts.

I roll my eyes at her mocking tone.

"I hope you don't think that with Alex is coming over
that you're exempt from finishing this movie with me. I
won't be able to sleep until I know how it ends. You know
this about me. If I watch a scary movie by myself without
seeing the bad man getting taken down in the end, I'll have
nightmares for a week."

I laugh despite the seriousness in her tone. "I would
never leave you in your time of need. Who knows what
would happen if I did. I would hate to wake up and find
you curled up in bed with me," I tease. "I'm not so sure how
Alex would feel about that."

I manage to sit through the rest of the movie with Jane
without her freaking out and hiding underneath the blanket that I gifted her after she ran out of pillows to throw
at me. Those I will keep in case I need any ammunition of
my own.

I'm so amped up over the fact Alex is coming over, the
remainder of the movie is a blur to me. I don't understand
why I am so nervous. I know I'm acting stupid, but I've never
hung out with him on my turf or with my friends before.
Just thinking about it has my body breaking out in a sweat
and my mind working overtime.

I'm busy cleaning up the kitchen and putting away what is left of our pizza when I hear a heavy knock on the front door. Sprinting around the kitchen like a mad woman on speed, I work fast to finish wiping down the counter tops before darting to my room.

Before I can finish finger combing through my hair and pinching come color into my cheeks, Jane has already abandoned her place on the sofa and is at the door letting him in. With the help of our paper thick walls, I listen in to their conversation as I hide out in my bedroom before taking the plunge and joining them in the living room. Okay, so maybe I'm being a coward by not facing him right away, but can you blame me? I can count on one hand the number of men who have been in my home. Alex being in my domain is a big deal to me. One I'm starting to have serious doubts about.

Pushing my uncertainty to the back of my mind, I place one foot in front of the other and force my feet to carry me to the living room. The moment I cross the threshold, all my nerves are put to rest. Jane and Alex are seated casually on the sofas, laughing and talking as if they have been best friends forever. My gaze pings back and forth between them in surprise. I don't remember ever seeing Alex so...so laid back. It's a good look on him.

The room stills as two sets of eyes seek me out, each holding a hint of amusement in their depths. Shoving away from the wall, I take a seat next to Alex after pushing away the heap of pillows I had stashed in the corner after Jane's earlier assault.

I open my mouth to break the silence when Alex chooses that moment to lean in toward me, his shoulder brushing seductively against mine. I suppress a shiver as he speaks.

"Sorry, it took so long. I tried to leave earlier, but I got held up by my lawyers," he says in a low rumble.

My interest is piqued. He's never talked about business around me before, despite me telling him more than enough about mine. Hell, he even knows the whole background of how we started with only a small loan we got from Jane's parents and a business plan written down on a napkin from our favorite coffee shop.

"Nothing bad I hope."

A muscle ticks in Alex's jaw as a weighted look takes over his handsome face. "Nothing that you need to concern yourself with." He links our hands together and places them in his lap as he leans back against the cushions, pulling me against his side. "This is what my lawyers get paid for, to handle those who think they can bully their way into getting more than they deserve. It won't be a problem for long," he says in a low, harsh voice that alarms me.

Jane shoots me a concerned look, and I answer with one of my own. I don't have a clue what has Alex so rattled, but from the unapproachable look on his face, now is not the time to dig any deeper into the subject.

For the next two hours, we watch re-runs of *Grey's Anatomy*, drink wine, and talk about insignificant things such as which TV doctor you would rather have stitch you up if you sliced open your arm, McDreamy or McHottie? It was a tie. I chose McDreamy and Jane chose McHottie. Alex refuses to break the tie with an answer, stating that we were being sexist and need to include a woman in the options.

With a yawn, Jane stands and excuses herself to go call David before she goes to sleep. I curl up on the sofa next to Alex while resting my head on his chest and enjoying the comfortable silence. Between the wine, the busy weekend, and the soothing sound of his heartbeat, my eyes fight a losing battle to stay open.

Pulling me across his lap, Alex sweeps me up, cradling me like a child and carries me to my bedroom. "Come on, baby, let's get you to bed," he whispers against my neck.

"Mmm," I answer followed with a yawn of my own.

Laying me on the bed, he strips me of my clothing with ease. I shiver as the air floats over my bare skin. Alex rumbles through my dresser before pulling a long nightshirt over my head. I sway in his arms, doing a horrible job at controlling my tired muscles as he dresses me. With little effort, he lays me back down on the bed, tucking me in like a child as he pulls the covers up to my chin.

I expect him to turn and leave, but instead he peels off his clothes. My eyes track his hands as he strips down to his boxers, his broad chest and abs on full display. Climbing into bed behind me, he pulls me close until we are chest to back. Feeling his heat seep into my own, has my body turning rigid against his.

Spending a night together after we've had sex is tolerable. Spooning together without sex dips into a gray area that makes me wary. I like keeping things simple, and somehow we have leaped past that line into dangerous territory. A place that will no doubt end with me having a broken heart and feelings for a man that will never be fully reciprocated. Spooning is something couples do, and no matter how you slice it, we are not a couple. I struggle to find the right way to tell him to leave without sounding like a crazy bitch.

"Stop overthinking it, Jessica," he murmurs, his voice rough with sleep. "Relax and close your eyes."

"How do you always know what I am thinking?" I ask, frustrated with his uncanny way of reading my mind. "It's creepy when you do that."

He laughs, and I can't help but liking the way his chest rumbles against me when he does it. "You are easy to read, my love." He places a soft kiss on my shoulder.

Clearing my mind, I cuddle further into his embrace and let the sleepy fog invade my senses. I drift off feeling content and happier than I have in a long time.

****

"Rise and shine, baby doll."

My eyes flutter open to find Jax sitting beside me on the bed. He is staring down at me with a big, know-it-all grin and sheer amusement dancing in his beautiful eyes. I scowl back at him. Why is he so perky this early in the morning?

I sit up slowly as the previous night's events roll through my mind. My gaze flickers around my room expecting to find Alex snooping through my things. Instead, I find a note laying on the pillow where he lay. An emotion I refuse to acknowledge assaults me when I realize he left without saying a word. I glare at the note with distaste. *Isn't leaving a note like a Dear John thing?*

Jax reaches over and thumps the note. "In case you were wondering, lover boy left early this morning, soon after I arrived to drag Jane off to the gym with me. We talked a bit. He wasn't as unpleasant as I previously pegged him to be. I dare say he's growing on me."

I hit him in the chest with my pillow. Laughing at the 'oomph," sound he makes. "You make him sound like a fungus," I accuse, doing a horrible job at hiding my smile. "What time is it?"

"A little after seven o'clock."

"Shit! I've overslept. Why didn't you wake me sooner?" I fight with my sheets and try to unwrap them from around my feet. With one leg free, I hobble out of bed only to stumble and end up falling flat on the floor. Of all mornings to sleep late this is the worst possible day I could have chosen.

"What's the big hurry today?" Jax asks while helping me off the floor. I can hear the humor in his voice and see his chest rising and falling with silent laughter at my predicament. Trying to be the bigger person, I chose to ignore it. At least for now. There is never an expiration date on paybacks. His is sure to come.

"I have a big meeting with a new client at eight-thirty."

"Okay," he says drawing the word out. "I've never seen you this worked up over a meeting before. What makes this one so special?"

"This is a good account. I mean a steak and lobster kind of account, not a chips and dip one like we normally get. I can't screw this one up. Now unless you plan on helping me, get out so I can get ready."

The look on Jax's face as I begin undressing is priceless. "Give me a head start before you do that," he protests, using one hand to shield his eyes as he darts to the door.

"Can't help it," I respond with a laugh. "You keep talking, and it's slowing me down."

"Go shower and make yourself pretty while I get your coffee ready and prepare you a breakfast meal to go," he says blowing me a kiss before he shuts the door.

"You are the best, Jax." I sprint to the shower, stripping off the rest of my clothes along the way.

The spray of the hot water cascades over my body as I methodically scrub all the important parts. I usually take my time and enjoy my showers, but time is not a friend of mine at the moment, so I hurry along, taking what could be the fastest shower known to mankind. Without enough time to blow dry my hair, I decide to towel dry it and spray some product in it to keep the humidity from turning it into a frizzy mess.

Yanking out my favorite red silk, sleeveless blouse and a black pencil shirt from the closet, I throw them on and cinch it at the waist with a black and gold belt. I have this secret obsession with wearing red to business meetings. The color reminds me of power and gives my confidence a much-needed boost. Studying my shoe options, I settle on a new pair of black open-toed Jimmy Choo stilettos I splurged on the last time Jane and I went to the mall. They might not be the most sensible option, but I love how they make my calves appear lean and sleek. Plus, who can say no to Jimmy Choo?

After adding a little mascara to my lashes, lip gloss to my lips, and a pinch of blush, I am ready to go with ten minutes to spare. Not bad if I do say so myself. Rushing into the kitchen I collect my paperwork along with the coffee and bagel smeared with cream cheese Jax so sweetly prepared for me. Taking a moment to collect myself, I sit down at the bar and use my last measly five minutes to chat with my two best friends.

"I need details," Jane demands the moment my ass touches down on the stool. "Did you manage to get any sleep or did that man of yours keep you busy all night?" I turn to give her the middle finger when I realize she is still busy rummaging through the sofa cushions in search of her car keys. I swear the girl would lose her head if it were not attached.

A little smile slips onto my face as I think about my night with Alex. I shrug as if last night was no big deal while trying to hide my smile. "I slept just fine, thank you very much. And for future reference, Alex is not my man." I scrunch up my nose as I try and think of the right word to describe what he is to me. Fuck buddy sounds too cheap and calling him my boy toy makes me feel like a slut.

"You are in denial," Jane accuses, followed by a triumphant "Ah ha" when she finds her car keys hidden under the couch.

Jax shoots me a quizzical look. "What did the note say that he left you?"

"Shit. I was in such a hurry earlier, I forgot all about it." Dropping my things on the bar, I scurry back to my room to retrieve it.

Returning to the living room with the note in hand, I waver on reading it out loud or keeping it all to myself. Judging by the glares I am receiving, there will be hell to pay if I shut them out. I open the note and laugh out loud when I see that he wrote it on my SpongeBob stationary my mom gave me last Christmas. I would have loved to see his expression when he found it.

I hold up the note so everyone can see. "It says. Enjoyed the sleepover. Looking forward to many more. P.S. Did you know you talk in your sleep? Don't worry, I'll keep your secrets safe."

I gawk at the note and re-read it three more times before throwing it in my purse and cursing Alex under my breath. Folding my arms, I give my friends a pointed glare. "Do I really talk in my sleep?"

"Yes," they answer at the same time, neither missing a beat.

My face screws up in disbelief. "Why haven't either of you ever told me this before?"

Jane shrugs, glancing at Jax for help, but Jax just shakes his head and leaves her to fend for herself. I frowned at them both. "You two suck," I grumble and then turn and gather my things back up.

A strange look passes between Jane and Jax, one that has me anxious and on high alert. I don't understand what is going on, but I have a feeling the joke is on me. The fact they both refuse to look me in the eyes only confirms my suspicions.

Glancing at the clock, I let out a long sigh and promise to revisit this matter at another time. Preferably when I can grill them separately and trick them into tattling on each other. With my breakfast in one hand and my papers shoved in the other, I usher my friends out the door and head to work.

We arrive at the office just in time for me to set out a variety of drinks and pastries before my meeting with a prominent photographer. Talk about putting the pressure on me. When the photographer walked in with a posse of five men in expensive suits, all wearing identical frowns, I came close to having an outright anxiety attack. Public speaking has always been a problem for me. Although six people do not make a large group, their impenetrable stares, and brash behavior still intimidated me.

All in all, the meeting went well and after answering several questions and presenting our portfolio they left with the promise to think it over and give us an answer within two days. I was pleasantly surprised when I found out they would also be attending the charity event I am going to with Alex tomorrow night. This function is looking better by the minute. I think it could be what we need to raise our business to the next level.

I will never admit he was right. I will take that bit of information to my grave.

Jane enters my office and plops herself down in the chair next to me. I continue to file away papers while waiting for her to speak up and tell me what is on her mind. She glances at her watch before nudging me with her arm.

"What's up?" I ask, my brow rising in question.

She gives me a pouty face that makes me laugh. "I'm starving. Let's go grab something to eat at that little bistro down the street. Jax said they served an amazing onion soup."

Studying my dwindling pile of papers, I give her a thumbs up. "Sure, why not. Let me grab my things, and I'll meet you at the elevator."

Jane yells over her shoulder as she rushes from my office. "Awesome. Don't dawdle around. My stomach is shrinking by the minute."

As I went about shutting down my computer and gathering my personal items, I glanced at the screen of my phone. Thumbing through my screens, I see that I missed one text from Alex saying good morning sexy, and one missed call from another private number.

I pause in the doorway and stare at my phone with a perplexed look on my face. *Who continues to call me from a private number?* My phone buzzes in my hand, and it frightens me so much that I jump, causing my phone to teeter in my hand. With quick reflexes, I manage to regain a good grip on it before it crashes to the ground. I let out a shaky laugh, surprised by how rattled my nerves are. With a glance at my phone, I see a new message from Jane.

Jane: Hurry your lazy butt up. I Need Food!!

Me: I'm coming. Hold your horses woman :)

Jane: I could eat a horse. I am that hungry.

Me: Good to know. I'm locking up know. Hold the elevator.

Chapter Ten

As we walk into the Bistro, I'm absentmindedly listening to Jane go on about a fight she and David had while my train of thought keeps going back to those strange private number phone calls I keep receiving. I didn't mention them to Jane because I thought it was a wrong number. Now I'm not so sure.

Following the bubbly hostess to our table, I take a seat across from Jane. With a sigh, I lean back in my seat and do my best to keep up with her story. I answer when I'm prompted to and smile at the appropriate times.

"Earth to Jess," Jane says waving a hand in front of my face. I blink, my eyes focusing back on her face. "You spaced out on me," she accuses, her face tight with annoyance.

I curse myself for being such a horrible friend, not to mention a crappy lunch date. Groaning, I give her my best puppy-dog eyes, hoping it will urge her to forgive me sooner rather than later. "I'm sorry. I didn't mean to. I've got something on my mind that I've been meaning to bring up to you and Jax. Truthfully, I thought I was making too much out of it." I shake my head and tap my fingers against the edge of the table as my nerves getting the best of me.

Jane reaches over and lays a hand over my tapping fingers, halting their motion. "You can tell me anything. What's freaking you out?"

"I've gotten a few missed phone calls from a private number on my cell phone. At first I thought it was a mistake, but it has happened more than once and they never leave a message." I give her a hard look. "That's odd, right?"

She waved a hand at me, gaining my full attention. "Sweetie, that could be anything. I admit it does sound odd. I'm sure there has to be a reasonable explanation."

"Like what?" I will her to come up with something that will settle my suspicions.

She frowns. "Well, it could be kids doing a stupid prank, or maybe we have a client who has a butt dial problem."

I shrug, giving her a yeah right look. "I don't think so. If it was a mistake, then why are they calling me from a private number?"

"I can't answer that." She gives me a small smile. "But I don't think anyone is out to get you or anything. We don't know that many people in Dallas, and the ones we do know are clients. As far as I am aware, they are all happy with us. Haven't had a complaint," she says, smiling. "Maybe all those scary movies I make you watch with me are getting to you." Jane's teasing helps to lighten the mood. I stick my tongue out at her before replying.

"Does that mean I'm exempt from the next one?" I make a big production of crossing both fingers and wishing for her to say yes.

"Never." She laughs as she swats me on the arm. "You can cross your fingers, all ten toes, and even those pretty eyes of yours and that still won't save you from me."

My lips curve into a soft smile as I relax back into my seat, feeling a hundred times better for finally talking to someone about the mysterious phone calls. There is nothing quite like the release you feel when you finally get your troubles off your chest and share them with your best friend.

Turning in my chair, I look around the room for someone who can take our order. "Jax better be right about this place having incredible food. If their service is anything to go by, then call me unimpressed. What does a girl got to do around here to get a drink?"

Zeroing in on a young waitress in the far corner who is busy flirting with a man at the bar, I catch her attention and motion for her come help us. As she walks our way, my eyes drift over the restaurant and land on someone I never thought I would see here. Alex is seated in a back corner booth looking devilishly handsome in a three-piece suit that screams come and get me. I push out my chair with the intention to go say hi until I notice he's not alone. The dipshit has company, and the kind that doesn't pee standing up.

"Jess, what's wrong? You just turned pale. Are you ill? Jessica? Talk to me. You're worrying me."

I try to answer her, but words evade me. Instead, I point to the corner behind her. I watch in stunned silence as she turns around to see what has got my feathers so ruffled.

"Mother fucker," she exclaims. "Who's the blonde bimbo?"

"No, clue. I can't get a good look at her from this angle," My blood begins to boil. From my vantage point, I can only see the back of her head. A head that is too close to Alex's to be just a friend or work acquaintance. I move in my seat, my eyes never leaving them as I watch, trying to get a look at her face. When she finally turns, and her face comes into view, a flash of red covers my vision as my temper flares to life. I immediately recognize her from the photo at Alex's house. The one hanging in his bedroom. She is the woman posed in the picture with his family.

What is she to him? The question keeps repeating in my head like a bad record.

Our waitress reluctantly saunters over to our table, and I'm thankful as Jane jumps to my rescue and orders for the both of us. Food is the last thing on my mind right now. My appetite has diminished, leaving a thick knot is taking up permanent residence in my chest. The two of them seem to be in a deep conversation, one I would give anything to be a participant in. I cringe every time she touches him. Whether it's a simple caress of his arm or a stroke on his hand, I want her to stop doing it. There is an intimate familiarity with the way they react toward one another.

Despite my ire with Alex, my traitorous eyes give him a studious glance. He looks handsome dressed in an elegant, dark-gray suit paired with a light-blue dress shirt and a silver tie. He could be the poster guy for every girls' wet dream.

Jane gives me a concerned glance. "Do you want to go over and throw water in his face or would you rather leave?"

I shake my head and push back the hoard of emotions threatening to bubble to the surface. "I'm not running away. I didn't do anything wrong. He did."

"Honey, you don't know who she is yet. It could be something as innocent as a work lunch."

"The day I let a man touch me the way that girl is touching Alex, is the day pigs fly. You don't touch a man like that unless you've already gotten naked with him. That girl," I hiss pointing in their direction, "knows him intimately. We promised to be exclusive, and from what I see right now, he has broken that agreement."

"Just wait till you get the full story before you go all crazy on his ass," Jane urges, giving me a pleading look that has me rolling my eyes. Angry with myself for showing how hurt I am, I pull my cell phone from my purse and begin typing.

"What are you doing?" Jane asks. Reaching over the table she takes a peek at my phone.

"I'm sending him a text asking him where he is. If I am blowing this out of proportion, he will openly tell me about his lunch date. If I'm right and he is a cheating pig, he will lie through his fucking teeth."

"If he is stupid enough to cheat on you, then he is an idiot who does not deserve you," she says sourly.

I nod lamely, not trusting my voice at the moment. I might talk a tough game right now, but inside I feel my heart fracturing.

Me: Hey babe, what are you doing?

I lean down in my seat and watch as his phone beeps. Pulling it out of his pocket, Alex stares at it for what feels like forever before texting back.

Alex: Busy with work. Can I call you later?

Me: Sorry to bother you. Are you at the office?

Alex sighs and glances over at the woman seated next to him. He looks as if the weight of the world is on his shoulders. For the briefest of moments, I almost feel sorry for him. Then I glance at his companion, and my anger rushes back, fueling my need to find out who she is and why she is with him.

Alex: Dinner tonight?

I glare at my phone as I bite on my bottom lip. It's not a flat-out lie, but he isn't dishing out the truth either. A lie by omission is still a fucking lie in my book.

Me: No thanks. I already have plans.

Alex's date is getting testy. I don't think she likes being ignored. He pushes a hand through his hair, his mouth pressing into a hard line. The blonde reaches out to him, running her hand across his forehead as she pushes away a few strands of hair that have fallen into his eyes. It takes everything in me not to run over there and slap the bitch's hand away. Why can't she keep her damn hands to herself?

Alex: What plans do you have and whom are they with?

Me: It is none of your concern. Enjoy your "work". Don't forget stop and eat, I would hate for you to work through lunch.

I place my phone down as our meal arrives. With a push, I slide my phone across the table to Jane, letting her read our exchange for herself. Her eyes darken with concern. I hate the gnawing feeling of jealousy that is flowing through me.

My concerns about him being a playboy like Travis are coming true.

Tired of hearing my phone continuously beep, I place it on vibrate and stuff it back in my purse. I can only read so much of his half-truths and pathetic attempts at dissuading my curiosity before I lose my mind. I pick at my food and keep a fake smile plastered on my face, not wanting to act like seeing him with someone else is tearing me up inside.

My acting skills must be lacking, because not ten minutes into our meal Jane calls our waitress over and has our untouched meals removed and boxed up to go. Throwing some cash on the table we quietly leave before he has a chance to spot us and head back toward the office.

My phone is buzzing so much you would think I had a handful of vibrators stashed in there. There is no telling how many missed calls and messages I have by now. I refuse to look. If I do, I'll be compelled to read them. I want to get home and sort out my thoughts alone. In the back of my mind I know there is a chance that I am overreacting, but that does not stop me from feeling betrayed. Even if his lunch date with the handsy bombshell was legit, he kept it from me.

As we pull back up to work, I shake my head and regain my focus. Climbing out of the car, I catch up to Jane before she heads inside. "I don't have any other meetings today so I unless you need me, I'm going to catch a cab and head on home."

"No, you go on home, rest, and drink a large glass of wine. I need to finish some paperwork before I can leave, and then I will come and join you." She gives me a reassuring hug. "Sweetie, you need to talk to him before you jump to conclusions," she says, her voice turning serious.

I nod my understanding and return her hug before walking to the curb and hailing down a cab. Giving him my address, I lean my head against the window and look out at the cloudless sky. Heeding Jane's advice, I pull out my phone and read through the dozens of text messages Alex sent, each one of them more frantic and desperate than the last.

Alex: Of course it is my concern. Why are you being cryptic?

Alex: Answer me, Jess!!

Alex: Damn it, Jessica. You are scaring me. Why are you shutting me out?

Alex: Where are you? I need to talk to you. Yell at me and call me names, anything is better than this silence.

Alex: I'm coming to find you, and when I do, we are talking. Fuck that, I am spanking you first then we will talk.

They just continue on from there. With shaky fingers, I type him out a quick text in hopes of gaining a few hours before I have to face him. Knowing Alex, he is already pulling favors and combing the city looking for me. Or maybe, he will have one of his hired flunkies to do it while he takes his lunch date back to his place and screws her. I cringe, hating the idea of him being with someone else.

Me: I'm fine. I'll call you later, and we can talk then.

Alex: No! Where are you? I need to see you.

Me: Not happening. I need some breathing room. I'll call you later.

Control freak.

****

A consistent loud thumping pulls me from a deep sleep. Disoriented and tired, it takes me a few minutes to sort out where I am. After getting home, I indulged in a long, hot shower before downing a glass of wine and curling up on my bed for a nap.

Wiping away a spill of drool from my lips, I haul myself out of bed and answer the door. There is no need to guess who is on the other side. The shouting of my name and the angry voice behind it is a dead giveaway. The moment the lock is free from the door, it flies open taking me by surprise and pulling a scream from me. Acting on instinct, I retreat to the safety of the living room.

My wide eyes collide with his menacing ones as Alex stalks my way. I lick my lips nervously as I take in his state of disarray. He is still wearing the same beautiful suit he had on earlier except now he is sans jacket, his shirt is encased in wrinkles, and his tie is undone and hanging loose around his neck. If anything he looks sexier than before. Standing in my doorframe, his darkened eyes bore down on me like a lion closing in on its prey.

His brow arches. "Why in the hell have you been ignoring me today?" His tone is harsh as he saunters towards me, kicking the door shut behind him. His gaze travels down my body, hungrily taking in the tiny camisole and boy shorts I changed into before lying down.

A riot of sensations warms my body, and the need to go to him assaults me. I fight against it. Blinking away the haze of lust, those warm sensations morph into anger as I remember why I came home and what I was witness to at the Bistro.

Bristling, I ignore his question and instead ask a few of my own. "How was your work today? Did you find it productive? Did it leave you feeling satisfied?"

Alex's mouth sets in a grim line. "It was manageable until I got your texts. After that, the rest of the day went to hell."

I shrug with indifference. "Sorry if I inconvenienced you," I answer, my voice dripping with sarcasm.

Alex's forehead wrinkles as he frowns at me. I open my mouth to tell him off, but he cuts me off with a hard glare. "I've been out of my mind trying to reach you. I went to your office, your home, and no matter how many times I called or texted, you ignored me. I want to know what the hell that was all about today?" he demands, his tone hard and pressing.

My back stiffens as I absorb the anger he is throwing my way. I gaze at him, shocked he has the audacity to yell at me after the stunt he pulled today. I glower at him. I try and play it cool and detached, but he's pushed me too far.

"Did you enjoy your work lunch at the Bistro today? You should try their spinach salad. I hear it is delicious." His frown deepens as I continue. "The blonde who was draped all over you sure seemed to enjoy herself. Is she a new toy or a spare you keep around?"

The air shifts along with his entire demeanor. Long gone is the impulsive spitting madman; in his place is a controlled, seductive beast. His eyes smolder as they meet mine and hold them captive. "You were at the Bistro today."

"Jane and I went for lunch. I remember seeing her before. In a family photo you have hung in your bedroom." He smiles sadly as I talk and never intervenes or tries to stop me, so I continue. "She doesn't have any of your family features. She pretty in a delicate kind of way." I swallow hard. "Who is she?" My voice breaks in the end, and at this moment I hate him for making me feel vulnerable.

Pushing off the doorframe, he stalks towards me, his strides steady and determined. With nimble fingers, he works at the buttons on his clothes, undressing himself with each step he takes, leaving a trail of clothing in his wake. It takes a moment for my brain to kick into gear, and when it does I retreat further into the living room.

My heart rate spikes as I take in every inch of his glorious muscular form. Swallowing hard, I try and ignore the eye candy in front of me and hold on to my anger as I address him. "I don't need a hard fuck, Alex. I need answers."

In my hasty retreat, I don't realize the couch is behind me until my calves bump into it. I have no escape. Alex grins knowingly as he saunters over to me, wrapping his arms around my waist and pulling me flush against him. My gaze drifts on its own accord, admiring his body and hard arousal as it tents the thin cloth of his boxers.

Lifting his hand, he lightly traces the outline of my jaw and down to my chest until he reaches the hem of my camisole. This is the point where I should push him away. I need to stop him, and yet, the words never leave my lips. I can't move. It's as if my feet are encased in thick concrete blocks, holding me prisoner where I stand. Gripping my camisole, he lifts it over my head in one swift motion leaving me standing in nothing but my small boy shorts.

I shiver as the cold air hits my skin. Before he can do more, I speak up. "Answers first, Alex."

He sighs and closes his eyes. I can tell he's fighting an internal battle; one I choose to wait out. After what feels like forever he finally lets me in and talks to me. "Her name is Lexy Brill and she is an old family friend. I've known her for as long as I can remember. Our families grew up together and have always been very close. She called earlier and asked me to meet her for lunch so we could go over some outdated contracts and agreements that we're both involved in."

Lexy. Where have I heard that name before? I rack my brain trying to remember and then it hits me like a ton of bricks. She's who he was on the phone with that morning in his office when I snuck out and caught a cab home. I don't remember a whole lot about their conversation but I do know he wasn't happy. I think it has something to do with a contract they were trying to get updated.

Maybe what he's saying is true. *God, I hope so.*

I purse my lips. The urge to give in and push this all behind us is strong, but a nagging feeling in the pit of my belly is urging me to dig deeper. I follow my gut instinct. "You both seemed very familiar with each other. Intimate even. Jax is one of my best friends, but I would never touch him the way she was doing with you."

His eyes burn into me, searing me down to my soul. His expression is so guarded, I can't fathom what he is thinking. Pulling back slightly, he drops one hand from my waist and runs it through his hair.

"If you can't be honest with me, then leave." My patience dwindles to practically nothing. I pull back further from him to show him that I am serious.

With reluctance, he spills more details, telling me things I would rather forget. "Lexy and I used to see each other romantically. It was a long time ago, and any feelings I once had for her are long gone. To call us friends now would be an exaggeration. We are more like acquaintances with similar business ties."

He scans my face trying to gage my reaction. I school my face into a blank slate, refusing to show him how much his words hurt. I've made a huge mistake. I let my guard down and gave him more of myself than I ever intended to. I hate the thought of him touching her in the same way he does me. The images of them together sear my mind, making me feel dirty and cheap. She is elegant, graceful, and obviously comes from money. She is everything I am not.

A lump is at the back of my throat making any attempt I might have to say something impossible. It doesn't matter, my mind is running rampant, never stopping at one thought long enough for to sink in. I've never been one for hiding my feelings well, and today is no different. Seeing the pain etched on my face, Alex intercepts me as his arms wrap around me in an embrace that is warm and welcoming. I inhale his familiar scent of cinnamon and vanilla allowing it to work its magic, as my muscles begin to relax and my breathing calms down.

His tone is sincere and honest when he speaks. "I don't want her, Jessica. I only want you. No one else."

I blink back unshed tears. I want to believe him, but I'd heard similar words from Travis, and look how that turned out. Cupping the back of my head, he claims me with his mouth. Caught up in the moment, I gasp as my feet leave the ground. He scoops me up in his arms, and I am carried down the hall to my bedroom and carefully deposited in my bed. Heat licks up my spine as Alex leans forward and tastes me through the thin layer of my panties. My fingers tangle in the thick strands of his hair as he continues to lick me, his tongue gaining velocity with each passing swipe.

"God, I love the way you taste. Tell me what I need to hear, baby," he says, his tone heavy with lust. "Tell me who owns this wet pussy?"

"It's yours, Alex," I say on a moan. "All yours," I repeat as a slow smile spreads across my face.

Slipping his thumb under the thin elastic, he slides my panties down. I lift my hips, giving him the access he needs while my eyes drift over his body, admiring the smooth skin and hard planes displayed before me. His body is a true masterpiece.

Dropping my panties on the floor, he stands and proceeds to push his boxers down over his hips. His glorious V of muscles makes a grand appearance. My eyes drop lower, latching onto the sight of his rigid cock as it stands to attention. It juts out proudly, lying hard and thick against his stomach. I lick my lips in anticipation as heat coils low in my belly.

"I need you Alex. I need to feel you inside me," I plead.

My arousal and need for him escalates to an unbearable level as I watch him stroke himself. The visual of Alex's hand sliding up and down his length, while his hooded eyes stay on me, is an image I plan on storing away for when I have some alone time with Mr. Rabbit (my pink vibrator).

"Don't worry, baby. You will very soon, "he promised. "Lean back and prop yourself up on your elbows. Spread your legs wide apart for me." His strong voice leaves no room for arguments.

Emboldened by the heat of his gaze, I position myself to his liking. Moving between my legs, he begins raining kisses from my ankles to the curve of my knee, and up to my wet sex. My eyes fight to stay open as his hot mouth dances over my swollen clit, sucking the tight bundle of nerves with an intensity that has my body trembling.

"I'm going to make you come so many times you'll never question my feelings for you again. No doubts, baby. We are in this together. You're all mine, and I'm all yours."

Mine? Yours? Is it stupid to want that also? *Probably. Yes, definitely yes.*

I let out a whimper as his fingers shift through my sensitive folds. Desperate for more I arch into his touch. Answering my silent plea, two fingers spear my slick flesh. His expression is tense as his fingers drag in and out of my quivering sex, rubbing all the right spots and sending me over the edge. I come hard, screaming his name as my hips continue to move in rhythm with his unmerciful strokes.

"That's one," he murmurs. His soft breath a sensual caress on my hypersensitive flesh.

Slipping a finger through my sensitive tissue, he seeks out my g-spot, a place no man has ever bothered exploring before. With expert manipulation, he presses on it, rubbing it in a way that makes my body weep and bow to his ministrations. His name is on my lips, coming out in pants through my ragged breathing. When the pressure in my core soars to an all-time high, his tongue darts out and flicks my swollen clit, the resolute strokes of his tongue is my undoing. A powerful orgasm rips through me. I come hard. With my back arched, I scream out incoherent words, my voice sounding labored, and nothing like my usual self.

"That's two," Alex murmurs, his voice sounding strained.

I close my heavy eyes as I ride out the blissful tremors racing through me. Giving me no time to come recoup, Alex stands and pulls my hips to the edge of the bed. Without any preamble or warning, he thrusts into me. My core is so wet he slides in easily, his cock sinking in deep. I moan in pleasure and let my legs fall apart as our bodies move on their own accord, slapping against each other in a harmonious rhythm. There is nothing sweet or sensual to our movements, only raw, animalistic thrusting, and grunting, each of us taking what we need and giving what we can.

"Alex..." I lace my arms around his neck as his cock pounds into me, my body inching up the bed with each powerful thrust. On another scream, my nails dig into his back as I scratch and mark his beautiful skin. He moans against me and eggs me on, getting off on the mixture of pain and pleasure as much as I am.

"You fit me perfectly, baby," he groans. I smile into the crook of his neck. This is exactly what I needed from him. I don't think I will ever tire of having sex with Alex. No man has ever met my needs the way he does.

A familiar tingling takes root within me. "Alex, please..." My voice breaks. I don't know if I can take anymore. I'm exhausted but in the best way possible. My legs ache as if they have run a marathon, my pussy is overstimulated, and my poor arms are close to resembling weak noodles.

Can you die of too many orgasms?

"Hang on, baby." With a tilt of his hips, Alex ruthlessly hammers into me, claiming new depths and sending my senses into overdrive. My hands grip his shoulders as his mouth latches onto my neck, sucking hard and no doubt, marking me again. He consumes me. With his breath searing my skin and marking my soul, I fall apart.

I scream his name as my muscles clamp down around him, my hips grinding into his as he follows me over with a grunt, his cum coating my insides.

We lay in a tangle of limbs, our heartbeats beating wildly. I have no energy to move, so I don't. Instead, I stay tucked under his arm, enjoying the feel of our skin slick against each other as my breathing begins to regulate. In the silence, I can't stop myself from second guessing all my previous decisions. I'm screwed, that much I do know. I've gotten in too deep with Alex. My feeling for him are too strong to ignore. Losing him would feel like losing a piece of myself. And that is the most frightening thing of all.

With a twist of his body, Alex propels himself on top of me, his knees on either side of my waist as he straddles my hips. Taking my chin in his grip, he bends down and holds my face within inches of his own. "Listen to me, Jess," he orders, his tone holds an edge that makes me wary.

My eyes narrow as they lock onto his stormy green ones. "Stop always overthinking everything. What is happening between us can be whatever we want it to be. No one can dictate that for us. If you need to go slower, we will. If you want to speed up, I'm all for that too. If labels bother you, then we won't use them. To hell with everyone else's expectations. You got me?"

I let out a slow breath. With a few simple words, he stole away the anxiety eating away at me. My shoulders sag with relief. I nod a simple yes, not trusting my voice at the moment.

"Don't shut me out, Jessica." He says his forehead resting against mine. "Promise me that, babe. I can't stand the thought of losing you."

There is a raw vulnerability in his voice that takes me by surprise. My heart melts with the realization Alex is as lost in me as I am in him. I pepper his mouth with kisses before moving down to his jaw and throat. Reaching the tender side of his neck, I wrap my lips around his skin and suck on it with the same intensity he used. Pulling back, I study it was a satisfied grin.

Chuckling, Alex reaches up and touches the dark-red mark. Blinking at me, he shakes his head. "I like you marking me. I also like that you got jealous over me today."

"I didn't like her touching you," I admit, stroking my thumb across his lips. Kissing him softly, I stroke my tongue against his.

His eyes lift, holding a tenderness in them I have never seen before. "She won't ever do it again. I promise you, baby, from here on out, it's just you and me."

I try and smile, but a yawn sneaks up on me and ruins the action. I can't remember the last time I've been this tired and truly fucked. I think my girly parts might be in need of a mini-vacation after tonight. Lord knows, they are going to be sore tomorrow.

Chapter Eleven

I wake to the sound of a voice laughing outside my bedroom. Several voices to be exact. Blinking against the soft light filtering through my window, I give my tired and sore muscles a good stretch before rolling out of bed. Wrapping my robe around myself, I pad into the kitchen where I am brought up short at the sight before me. I feel like I have awoken in a scene straight out of the Twilight Zone. Blinking my eyes, I watch as Jane, Alex, and Jax all sit together around the breakfast table talking and laughing as friends while munching on donuts.

My eyes drop to the heap of gooey goodness with distrust. *How could one pastry cause so much havoc in my life?*

"Morning, baby doll," Jax calls out. Alex makes a face, clearly not approving of Jax's nickname for me.

"Good morning," I answer back.

I lean against the granite countertop and eye everyone around me while trying to work out what the hell is going on. I should be happy to find them all hanging out together. I mean, I am happy, but I am also confused and very much on guard. "What's going on?" I ask, trying to keep my tone light. "Why do you all look like you just robbed a bank or something?"

Jane and Jax let loose a string of giggles and snorts, none of which does anything to ease my nerves. I glance around the room relieved to find that our clothing is no longer littering the living room floor. I hope Alex was the one to clean it up and not either of my giggly friends. They would never let me live it down.

Alex passes by me on his way to the coffee pot. Dressed in a pair of low-hung, ripped jeans that hug his hips and a T-shirt with some band name on it I've never seen before. I assume that either Carson made an early appearance this morning and brought over some extra clothes or he was smart and kept an extra set stored in his car. Either way, he looks downright sexy with his mussed bed hair and scruffy jaw.

Against my better judgment, I grab a glazed donut as I take a seat beside Jax. Tearing off a bite, my tummy grumbles loudly, reminding me that I didn't eat near enough yesterday. I devour my donut while arguing with Jax over his sister's right to choose who she dates without his interference. Jax can't stand her newest love conquest and thinks she could do better. In truth, I don't think he will ever approve of anyone she brings home. He's a great big brother but overly protective. No one she chooses will ever be good enough in his eyes.

Alex joins us, taking the seat beside me and sliding over a freshly brewed cup of coffee my way. My eyes roll back into my head as I inhale the delicious, warm smell of coffee beans and cream, making my taste buds ache for its velvety smooth flavor. Sipping on my favorite concoction, Alex slips an arm around my shoulder as he pulls me to his side. I let out a happy sigh as his warmth wraps around me. I hate to get my hopes up, but I wish all mornings could be like this. With everyone I love all in one room together, my heart swells. For the first time ever I feel complete.

Shaking out of my reverie, I kick my leg under the table and give Jane a little nudge with my foot. "I hate to bust up the party, but if we're going to make it to work on time, then we need to get ready."

Jane's back stiffens and before she can hide it, I catch her glancing over at Alex with wide, anxious eyes. I turn to him, my eyebrows scrunching as I give him my best you're-an-idiot look.

Before I can interrogate him, Jane speaks up. "You should probably go shower and get dressed. Wear something comfortable. We have a full day at the spa planned for us," she says, her eyes highlighted with excitement. "If you make me late for my deep-tissue massage, I might hurt you. So, get off your cute ass and go get ready."

"What about you talking about? Today is Tuesday. That is a typical day in the week, which means we have work to do, and clients to please."

"Not today," she argues with a shake of her golden hair. "I've already re-arranged all of our appointments, so we now have the whole day free to enjoy ourselves. I even talked Jax into joining us." She is practically bouncing up and down with glee as she speaks.

The conversation makes me smile, and I can't deny the excitement I feel at playing hooky and enjoying the day with Jane and Jax. I have to wonder though what part Alex has in all of this. I take a sip of my coffee, eyeing him thoughtfully over the rim.

Snuggling into his side, I lay my head on his shoulder. "Are you behind this?" I ask coolly.

"I might have helped a little," he answers with a smile.

A little my ass. His name is written all over this un-prompted day of leisure. My eyebrows rise in question, willing him to fess up and tell me all his secrets. Well, maybe not all of them at once, but I think this is a good place to start.

"I own a hotel and spa downtown. I called and made arrangements for you and your friends to enjoy a day of pampering. It will give you a chance to unwind before the big charity event tonight."

I'm impressed by his kindness toward my friends. Just when I think I have him, all figured out he goes and shows me another side of himself I didn't know existed. "Thank you, Alex. You didn't have to do that, but I'm glad you did," I say honestly.

He shrugs as though it's no big deal, and maybe for him it isn't, but for me it's huge. I can't remember the last time I took a day off. A sliver of excitement rolls through me at the thought of a spa day with my friends.

Leaning down he lays a chaste kiss on my shoulder. "I hate to leave, but I need to get back home and get ready for the day." Standing in a fluid motion, he says a quick good-bye to his partners in crime before gathering his things and heading toward the door with me in tow.

Reaching the entryway, I am caught off guard when Alex snags an arm around my waist and pulls me against his chest. With his hand cupping my face, he tips my head back and buries his face in the curve of my neck. He licks at my collarbone as he works his way up, taking my mouth in a brutal kiss. On a gasp of surprise his tongue dips in and turns what should've been a simple kiss goodbye into a scorching, all-consuming, panty-dropping mind-fuck. I arch into him, eating up all space between us as I groan into his mouth and press against his lips harder.

I swear he has ruined me. The feel of his body rubbing up against me, the minty taste of his mouth as it claims me, and that delicious scent of cinnamon and vanilla that is singularly all him; has become an addiction my soul craves like a junkie craves meth. It's all too much, and yet it's somehow just right.

How the hell did this happen? When did I fall in love with Alex Harlow? My mind is in a tailspin as I continue to stroke my tongue against his, loving the way he always kisses me like it's the last time he'll ever see me.

"Fuck, you taste good." He pulls back from my mouth and leans against the wall, holding me tightly to his chest. I smile when I hear his heart beating as fast as mine, matching beat for beat.

Giving me a wicked grin, he rubs my swollen lips with the pad of his thumb. "If I don't get out of here now, I never will."

I draw in a huge breath at his words. "Why not?" I challenge.

He smiles a real smile; the kind that spans his whole face. "Don't tempt me, beautiful," he warns. "Given the chance, I will happily carry you back to your room and fuck that tight pussy of yours until you're begging for mercy."

I tilt my head up and trace his lips with my tongue. "What's wrong with that? Sounds like a great plan to me."

The lengthening of his cock against my stomach and the moan that hisses through his teeth has me thinking I won this round. That is, until he pushes me back, forcefully putting distance between us. He makes a show of adjusting the large bulge now tenting his loose jeans "You're killing me, babe."

I grunt in response, not liking how far away he is from me. "I promised Jane this morning that I would not interfere or spoil your plans with her. She threatened to smash my balls in and make them into shish-kabobs if I did."

My lips pinch together in an attempt not to laugh. I love Jane like a sister. Through thick and thin that girl has stayed by my side. She has always been there for me, and I will always be there for her. The image of her threatening the big, bad Mr. Harlow with physical violence is hilarious. I clamp a hand over my mouth trying to stifle my surging giggles. My attempt is fruitless as a few chuckles escape my lips.

Alex sighs and glances down at this watch. "I've got to run. Enjoy your day. Everything at the spa is covered, so take advantage and get any treatment you desire. Lunch will be delivered to you whenever you're ready, and I'll have the car sent to pick you up at four o'clock."

I stare in awe, feeling undeservingly spoiled. I want to wave off his generosity, but I've learned by now that my protests will go unanswered. The last thing I want to do is disappoint my friends, and another argument with Alex over something so trivial would be pointless.

"I will try and find a way to thank you later," I say with a coy smile.

He holds me with his gaze. His features appear intense and troubled as if he is internally fighting something. What? I have no idea. In a blink, his mood shifts as quick as it had come, and he is once again sporting a devilish smile. His mood swings are erratic enough to give someone whiplash. Leaning down, he presses a tiny kiss to the tip of my nose, gives me a wink, and then darts out the door.

Looks like Mr. Moody is back.

I join my friends in the living room to find them cleaning up the remnants of our breakfast and sorting everything we need for our day. Jane catches my attention as she rounds the corner, her arms full of clothes and what-nots.

"Get your ass moving, or we will be late. I wasn't joking about getting a massage today." She stands with a hand on her hip, giving me a pointed look. "I'm giving you fifteen minutes. Then we are leaving no matter what. If I have to drag you out of here in your panties and bra, I will. No shame in my game," she threatens.

Taking Jane's threat seriously, I rush to my bathroom and take a quick shower. Dressed in a pair of shorts and a light-yellow tank top, I brush my teeth, add a dash of powder to my nose, and a bit of pink balm to my lips. With no time to spare, I throw my hair up into a messy bun before rejoining my friends in the living room.

Since we first took the plunge and formed our business endeavor, Jane and I haven't had the luxury of long holidays or many off days. The few we have had always ended with us either cleaning the apartment, gaining some much-needed sleep or obsessing over an upcoming gig. None of which I would call relaxing.

As I am busy switching out of my carry-everything bag to one that is more practical, I can literally feel Jane's eyes boring into the back of my skull. Tilting my head in her direction, I take in her puzzled expression and raise my brows in question. "What's the deal, pickle?"

Jane blinks in confusion at my question, and I can't help but laugh. Her blank expression is too hilarious.

She points to my cell phone that is lying on the table. "Are you actually planning on taking that with us today? I know we should be responsible businesswomen and all, but I'm feeling selfish. I don't want to take a chance on anything ruining our one day of fun."

I frown as I think it over. "I get your point, but what if we have an emergency and need help."

"I'll bring my phone in case that happens. It's not hooked into the work line, so there is no chance of anyone calling and expecting us to drop everything we are doing to run and make them look beautiful."

I want to disagree and say no, but the sad pout Jane is giving me is too hard to say no to. When Jax joins in gives me his puppy dog eyes, I throw my hands up in surrender. My friends are ridiculous. Tossing my phone back into my room, I slide on a pair of shoes and follow everyone out the door.

****

The spa was amazing. I'm relaxed and my muscles are limp noodles. The day began with a deep-tissue massage that was followed up with a mani-pedi. Afterward, Jane and Jax went to indulge in a mud bath while I had a team of women who helped me with my hair and makeup for tonight. It was weird having someone else do my face, but in the spirit of things, I gave in to the moment and let it go.

Alex did not spare a penny on anything. We had a personal hostess and team of attendants who waited on us the whole time. It was like we were superstars.

Jax acted like a big baby when it came time to get his feet scrubbed. He moaned and groaned the entire time which only enraged Jane and led to her getting revenge. During Jane and Jax's mud bath, Jax made the mistake of falling asleep in the tank. Jane smeared mud all over his face and took candid pictures of him which she posted on his

Facebook wall with the caption, Prissy Boy. His phone has been blowing up with calls from all his guy friends. Needless to say, they are laughing at him and after a unanimous vote, deemed prissy boy his new nickname. I don't think the poor guy will ever live it down.

My whole body feels boneless by the time we arrive back home. Dragging my tired ass into the apartment, I contemplate taking a nap, but with little time before I need to get my ass in gear, I have to forfeit such a temptation. With a grunt of frustration, I throw the bag of lotions and creams I bought from the spa gift shop into my bathroom then go crawl onto the bed. I might not have time for the nap I desperately want, but I can at least rest my eyes for a few minutes.

Swaddled in a mountain of blankets, I'm seconds away from sleep when Jane's persistent voice drags me back to the land of the living.

"What now?" I glare at my friend. "What are you harping on about?"

"You so testy. I was asking if you've spoken to Alex yet?"

"No," I huff. Before I can think against it, I grab up a discarded book from my bed and throwing it her way. I know my actions are immature, but I am tired. "Why do you ask?"

Jane dodges the book and lets out a shriek of laughter. "When you do, please make sure you let him know I appreciated today. I had fun."

I smile at her statement and blow her a kiss. With all the ups and downs between she and David, it has been a while since I glimpsed Jane with a real smile on her face. "I'll call him now and thank him for the both of us."

Propping myself up on my elbow I lean over the side of the bed and pull my phone off the charger from the bedside table. Rubbing the sleep from my eyes, I swipe my finger across the screen and unlock it to find three missed calls and a new voicemail. I open up another screen to check the details of the calls. My stomach dropped as I studied the information. Two of the calls were from another private number, go figure, and one is from an unfamiliar number with the same area code as my old hometown.

A tsunami of emotion rolls over me as I sit there staring at my phone. The stupid blinking, voicemail icon taunts me to listen to it, but some part of me knows that whatever is on there is bad news. When I left my hometown, it was not on good terms. Travis did a remarkable job at dragging my name through the mud and the few friends I did have disappeared when our engagement fell through.

The only person I talk to from back there is my mom, and even that only happens once or twice a year. My mom and I have never had a good relationship, and truth be told, she was happy when I left. And then on top of all that I have to deal with more anonymous calls. It is wasn't for the business, I would change my number and call it a day, but that is not an option. Taking a calming breath, I push the voicemail button and listen as an all-too-familiar male voice rolls over the speakerphone.

I freeze in place as my heart kicks up and a cold sweat breaks over my skin. It's amazing how just hearing a person's voice can make your body relive a pain it once endured. That is what I am doing right now. Just hearing his voice has me feeling weak and pathetic like I once did. I haven't experienced this many conflicting emotions since I left Travis and moved away to college with the hopes of starting over.

Jane must not have been too far away. Within seconds she comes barreling into my room, eyes wide, and lips drawn into a petulant frown. She points down to my phone, glaring at it as if it's an evil device that can mysteriously make Travis appear. Her lips lifts in a sneer. "Is that who I think it is?"

My heart flutters wildly as I give her a shrug. "Umm...yes." How did everything get so turned around? I bite my lower lip between my teeth to stop it from quivering. "I don't understand how he got my number." Out of all the things running through my head, that is the one thing I keep coming back to.

Jane mumbled something under her breath about Travis being a brainless dick wad before giving me a sad look. "I don't know, sweetie. If he found out where we work than he could have gotten it from our messaging center or maybe your mom broke down and gave it to him."

I shake off the thought of my mom and Travis joining ranks. I might not be the apple of her eye but I can't imagine her doing something as sinister as teaming up with the likes of him. There was a time when the sound of Travis's voice made me feel safe and treasured. When things would get tense with my mom, he would be the first person I ran to. He was always there for me.

Now, hearing my name roll off his lips makes my skin crawl. His lies and betrayal tainted everything we ever had together. Since Alex came along, I am second guessing what love really is. I'm not even sure what Travis and I had was real or just an elaborate joke that I became the butt of in the end.

Several minutes have passed as we sit in a comfortable silence. Jane stares at her hands as she twines them together before reaching over and giving my arm a gentle nudge.

"Would you mind playing it one more time?" Without question, I hit play again.

Jess, it's me, Travis.

I'm sure you are surprised to hear from me. I remember how you hate random talks, so I will skip to the heart of this call. I miss you, ladybug. I hate how things ended between us. I messed up. I should have stood up to my dad and not let him spread those rumors about you. I know it was wrong, and for that I'm sorry.

I've thought a lot about it since you left. What I did was stupid and immature. Dad says I was just sowing my oats, but I know that is a cop out. I ended things with Trish for good. She was a mistake. She wasn't you, Jess. She could never be you. You and I were good together once. I know that if we work at it, we can get that back. I would like see you again. Just think about it. I'll call you back later.

I love you, ladybug.

Jane's eyes are as wide as saucers by the time the message finally ends. I lean back into the soft pillows and open my mouth to speak, but nothing comes out. I think I'm in shock. Obviously Jane is not having that same problem. She is spewing a long list of profanities that would make any biker or sailor a proud man.

"What the fuck was that about?" I bite back a grimace as I take in Jane's hostile tone and expression. Jane isn't one to get mad very often, but when she does you better watch out. She is like one of those super volcanoes you hear about on the science channel, quiet, inconspicuous, and deadly when disturbed.

"I don't know." I sigh as I shook my head. Out of all the people I thought might be trying to reach me, I never once thought it would be Travis. An unhappy client or an old flame of Alex's out for retribution made more sense. I let out a harsh laugh as his words replay in my mind. "Just hearing his voice again makes me feel dirty. He is off his rocker if he ever thought I would take him back."

Jane captures my hand, her grip tight as her eyes plead with me. "Please promise me that you won't call that ass wipe back."

"You don't have to worry about that. I feel nothing but disgust for him. Any part of me that once loved him died the day I found his dick shoved in that slut. The day I want Travis back is the day pigs learn to fly, and hell gets a skating rink."

I give Jane a forced grin and change the subject to something lighter and less mood shattering. We spend over an hour laying on my bed talking about the reasons behind David's lack of communication and Jax's abundance of nameless women. Our aimless chatter is exactly what I needed to help loosen the knot of tension that had taken root in my chest. I would never admit it to Jane, but hearing from Travis again after all this time has jarred me and brought back some unwanted memories and self-doubts.

Our conversation is brought to a sudden halt as my phone beeps. With a groan, I check my phone and find a new text from Alex.

Alex: I will pick you up at 6:00. Did you enjoy your day?

Me: It was wonderful. Thank you again.

Alex: If you're adamant about thanking me, I have a few ideas. Don't wear any panties tonight. I want full access to you at all times

Me: You can't be serious. There is no way I can attend an elaborate function pantyless.

Alex: You can and you will. I'll be the only one to know. See you soon, baby

Kinky bastard, I think as I throw my phone on the bed. The thought of going commando in a room full of potential, high-end clients is making my stomach revolt. I can't help but feel frightened. I understand the chance of anyone finding out is slim, but with the luck I've been having lately, I can see it happening.

Jane pinched my cheek, gaining me attention. "Why do you have that goofy grin on your face?"

I blush beet red as I imagine her expression if I told her Alex pressed me to skip out on wearing my panties tonight. Yeah, not going to happen. I might share my hopes, dreams, and many failures with Jane, but dishing on my sex life is out of the question. Every girl has to have a few secrets she keeps to herself. What Alex and I do under the sheets isn't up for discussion. At least not tonight.

I shrug and stick my tongue out at her. Not a mature response, but it does the job of distracting her. "Alex will be here soon, so I better get ready."

"Call me if you need any help."

Retrieving my garment bag out of my closet, I hang onto the door with one hand as I step into the gown, sans panties. I move as slow as a turtle in hopes of not messing up my hair and make-up. The spa did an outstanding job of curling and pinning up my hair, leaving out a few long tendrils to frame my face. Alex thought ahead and provided them with a photo of my dress so they would know what hair style and make-up would best compliment it. I'm embarrassed I never thought to do that myself, but then again

I'm not accustomed to attending such events. He is probably a pro at this by now. There is no telling how many he has under his belt.

Twirling around like a ballerina on a stage, I admire my gown in the mirror. I feel like Cinderella before the big ball, only this Cinderella has a kinky prince instead of a gentleman waiting for her. The gown I picked out is long enough to skim the floor with a high slit going up the side that shows a lot of leg. It's a sheath-style dress with a fitted halter top done in a dark silver color that sparkles when it catches the light. I fell in love with it at first sight. After slipping on my silver, rhinestone-encrusted stilettos, I call Jane in to get her opinion.

Strolling into my room, Jane lets out a low whistle as I do a little turn, letting her get a good look at my outfit. "You are a knockout, Jess. The slit is smoking hot." She winks at me. "I want your legs. They look killer in that dress."

I roll my eyes and despite the chill in the room, my cheeks warmed. "You don't think it's too much?" I ask with unease. "I feel like the halter part shows too much of my boobs. I don't want every man there thinking they are on the menu." I try for the umpteenth time to pull the fabric up but with the way the dress is made, it won't give an inch. "I don't want to look slutty."

"Honey stop doing that," Jane chastises, shoving my hands down to my sides. "I would never lie to you." I smile at the sincerity and honesty in her voice. "Trust me when I say you look incredible. I hope Alex ate his Wheaties tonight because he's going to be busy fighting guys off you with a stick. He's a lucky bastard to have you on his arm."

Our girlie moment is shattered by a loud knock on the front door. Jane clears her throat as she rubs the back of her neck. "You ready?" she asks giving me a questioning look.

My nerves get the best of me as I eye myself in the mirror one last time. Plastering a smile on my face, I give her a shaky nod. Linking my arm in hers, we leave the sanctuary of my room and head back to the front of the apartment. Walking around without panties on is unnerving to say the least. I subconsciously squeeze my thighs together, trying to stifle the heat blooming in my core.

How the hell am I going to last a whole night like this?

I hang out in the living room while Jane goes and answers the door. When Alex steps into the room, my breath hitches as a small smile tugs at my lips. My grin grows as my eyes roam over his body, admiring the way his black, custom-fitted tuxedo molds his physique. The dark-silver, button-down shirt he wore compliments my dress, making us look like one of those crazy couples who always wear matching outfits. As our eyes meet, the satisfaction gleaming back at me made my pulse jump.

"You look gorgeous, Jessica." Wrapping a hand around my waist, Alex leans down and places a kiss right behind my ear.

I stood mute for a long moment before trusting myself to speak. Once my pulse quiets, I gave him another quick perusal. "You look quite delicious yourself, Mr. Harlow. If you continue to stare at me like you want to devour me, we won't be making it to the event on time," I warn, my voice sounding huskier than normal.

Alex chuckles and nods once before stepping back and shoving his hands in his pockets. His eyes sparkle with mischief that has me on edge. "Before we go, I think your ensemble is missing something." I watch entranced as he pulls a dark blue velvet jewelry box from his pocket. With a flick of his wrist, it opens with a pop, revealing a stunning teardrop diamond necklace.

I didn't move, not that I could at the present moment. My weak legs shake as I stare at the sparkling necklace with an expression that could only be described as awe. Nervously, I reach out and finger the smooth diamonds. I don't know a whole lot about what makes one diamond better from the others, but seeing how clear and sparkly these were, I assume they were a good grade. Of course they would be; it's not like Alex would ever buy anything subpar.

Pulling my hand back, I attempt giving him an appeasing smile. My mouth dries. The glower Alex is sending my way is not the expression I had expected. *Crap.* "Um... The necklace is lovely." I give it one last glance before turning my head away. "I can't accept it, Alex. That is too expensive and extravagant a gift. I am more of flowers and chocolates type of girl," I joke trying to ease away the tension that is mounting between us.

He furrows his brows as he stares at me like I am a puzzle that needs sorting. Blowing out a deep breath, he spins me around and yanks me back. I let out an umph sound as my backside collides with his chest. His breath tickled my ear as he speaks, his tone firm and unyielding. "Stop overthinking everything, baby. This is a special night, and I am asking you nicely to wear this for me." He runs his thumb across my collarbone as he speaks. Desire explodes in my body. "Are you wearing panties, Jessica?"

I lean back and grind my ass against the prominent bulge growing in his pants. "No, Alex. No panties."

He moans in appreciation and places a soft kiss on my neck. I shudder in his arms as heat blooms at my core. With nimble fingers, he clasps the necklace around my neck. I wiggle in his arms, causing his erection to dig in farther, hitting me in all the right spots.

He spins me around, and I feel the weight of his eyes taking me in. "You're perfect," he says, the tension in his body leaving as his eyes darken. "Every time you feel your slick nectar pooling between your thighs tonight, I want you to think of me." I gasp as his fingers slide up the inside of my thigh, landing heavily on my bare mound. A wolfish smile curves his lips. A shiver runs down my spine as his finger drew circles on my clit. "I can't wait to feel your greedy, warm cunt wrapped around my cock when we get back tonight."

Fuck. Me. Chills erupt on my skin.

He moved slowly as he releases me. "We should be going." The depth of his voice made me want to beg him to strip and take me now. I bit my tongue and kept my mouth shut knowing tonight's event was more important than me getting off. I could wait a few hours for that. Maybe.

My smile fades. I busy myself by smoothing out my dress as I try to regain what little composure I have left—which isn't much.

"Lead the way, Mr. Harlow."

Chapter Twelve

The charity event has been a gold mine as far as business connections go. Over the last few hours, I've met several producers, a range of actors, and high-end magazine execs. Not to toot my own horn, but little old me set up an appointment for the end of this month with a new client. The gig is to work on the set of a commercial that will be shot over at the Cowboys stadium. As exciting as it is, I'm not delusional enough to think I did this all on my own. Having Alex by my side has opened doors that I never would have gotten within a mile of. Everyone here has been carving out time to come over and greet him. Alex is a business god among this crowd. All the men want to shake his hand, and all the woman want to fuck him.

Can't say I blame them.

Surrounded by a room full of elite and powerful people dressed to the nines I feel like a piece of Spam surrounded by a table full of caviar. To say I am out of my element would be the understatement of the century. Willing my hands to stop shaking, I take deep breaths as I admire my surroundings.

The event is being held in an elaborate ballroom in one of Dallas' premier downtown hotels. Whoever was hired to orchestrate the decor has an eye for detail. Between the dozen or so gold chandeliers adorned with crystals and pearls, the elegantly draped ivory chiffon ceiling panels, to the private, garden courtyard, rich, stone columns, and romantic, tealight candles positioned on every table, the ambiance can only be described as exquisite.

My only complaint of the night is the backstabbing women who keep throwing themselves at my date. I have no experience when it comes to dealing with catty women. If they're not shooting me death glares from across the room, they are boldly throwing themselves at him in front of me.

Who does shit like that? I get that Alex is the total package. Many women see him as a one-way ticket to the good life, but who in their right mind stoops so low as to hit on a man in front of his date?

Skanks, that's who.

The more he brushes off their advances, the harder they try and reel him in. It is embarrassing the lack of morals, not to mention pride, some women have. One pixy-faced woman with boobs made of pure silicone went as far as to rub her hand over his crotch when she thought I wasn't looking. Before I had a chance to think, I had her dainty hand restrained in a vise grip. Her face full of contempt mirrors my own. Chuckling through it all, Alex took over and has her escorted away.

I still have no clue what my next step was with her, but I'm almost positive that it went beyond inviting her for drinks later or complimenting her on her choice of plastic surgeon. I've never felt such a surge of rage or possession directed at another person as I did when she laid her manicured fingers on Alex. *My Alex!* It completely unnerves me. Hearing my name called draws me out of my head.

"Jess, would you like something to drink?" Alex asks steering us toward a large bar stationed at the back of the room. His eyes are intent as he watches my face, no doubt trying to read my expressions.

I quickly look away to cover the blush creeping up my neck. "Yes, that would be nice."

With his hand positioned on the small of my back, we make our way to a fully stocked, floor to ceiling bar where Alex orders two flutes of champagne. The bubbles tickle as they slide down my throat. Needing all the false courage I can get tonight, I finish off the drink in three large gulps before ordering another. Alex gives me a look that makes it clear he doesn't approve, but he never moves to stop me. Pushing back my inner bitch who itches to lash out and taunt him, I do the opposite. I act mature and take small sips so as not to get overly tipsy.

With his arm snaked around my waist, I naturally lean into his powerful body. My breath stutters as I try to concentrate on anything besides the heat of his body melding with mine. My attempt is unsuccessful. "So besides rubbing elbows with the uber rich and fighting off wanton women, what else is planned for the evening?"

His eyes soften as he gives me a playful smile. "We will greet a few more people and dance a bit. Later, when no one is looking, I plan on sweeping you out of here and having my way with you at my place." His arm slides up my back as his hand rests heavily on the nap of my neck. Tilting his head down, he whispers in my ear. "As much as I love seeing you in that dress, I enjoy seeing what's underneath it even more."

Licking my lips, I struggle for my next breath. My voice wavers as I speak. "Dancing is overrated. Are you sure we can't leave now?"

Gripping my neck like he owns me, Alex brings our faces within inches of each other. Our eyes hold as a flicker of emotion passes over his features. As he speaks, his minty breath fans my face. "Watch yourself, Jess. Play with the bull baby and you might get the horns."

Hearing Alex's warning has goosebumps skirting up my arms. "What does that mean?"

Closing the distance between us, Alex kisses my jaw. "When we have some privacy, I will show you." Pulling away he gives my bottom a playful slap. "Now play nice. There are a few more people I would like to introduce you to before we leave."

Linking my hand in his, I relax and allow him to lead me around the room.

For the last two hours, Alex has stopped and spoken to practically everyone we've come in contact with. Regardless of Alex being a gentleman and introducing me to every-one, I still felt like arm candy and stayed quietly in the background while he discussed the latest upcoming model or top business stock. I nod at all the right times while inwardly I'm bored to death.

While Alex is in deep conversation with a robust, balding man who is trying his hardest to sell Alex on a new digital magazine software program, I feel a slight tap on my shoulder. Glancing behind me, I'm surprised to find a handsome, thirty-something, blond gentleman with a devilish grin gracing his face. You know those moments when you see someone, and their face is familiar to you, but no matter how hard you rack your brain, you can't remember why or how you know them. That is what I'm going through right now.

Before I have a chance to place him, he speaks, his voice as strong and commanding as he is. "You are way too beautiful to stand on the sidelines. Care to dance?"

I stare at his outstretched hand and smile despite my trepidation. I've sought to dance since we first arrived, but Alex has been so wrapped up in mingling I've been ignored. My hand itches to meld with his, but my inner voice is screaming at me to stop and think this through. I glance back at Alex, only to find him entranced in whatever information Mr. Baldy is supplying.

Setting down my drink, I throw caution to the wind and take his outstretched hand. "I would love to dance," I say, trying to sound casual. Weaving through the throng of bodies we find a small clearance. With a not so gentle tug, he pulls my body against his. My body chills as his arms wrap around my waist, holding me much closer than I would prefer.

Keeping my expression cool, I pull back from his hold and place my hands flat on his chest in hopes of keeping some semblance of space between us. With a harsh laugh that reverberates through me, he ignores my resistance and pulls me tight to his chest.

"Don't worry, I don't bite. Unless you are into that sort of thing, then all bets are off." His gravelly voice skates down my body, and not in a good way, sending goosebumps over my flesh.

I swallow hard as my instincts kick in and my inner voice screams at me to go find Alex. "You might not, but I'm not so sure my date won't if he catches you dancing so close to me." I warn, giving his chest a hard push as I prepare to fight him off if necessary. Gaining a few respectable inches between us, I relax with the knowledge that the song will soon be over, and I will be able to use that time to make my escape.

"I don't remember ever seeing you at one of these functions before. What is your name, sweetie?"

I ignore the "sweetie" remark and give him a curt answer. "Jessica Grayson. And you would be?"

He clears his throat as his eyes light up with humor. "My name is Derrick Johnson."

I give him a lopsided smile as his name sets off a symphony of bells in my head. My questions come out rushed. "Derrick Johnson from the Dallas Cowboys? That Derrick Johnson?" I am sure my eyes are bugging out of my head, but I can't help it. It's not every day you meet an up-and-coming football star.

I don't know much about football, but I've read amazing things about this man. The latest news flash was about how he was recently traded to Dallas from another team up north. Football is like a cult in Texas. Even if you don't follow the game, it's engrained in you from birth to love the sport. The whole city of Dallas is expecting Derrick to turn things around for the team and lead them to victory.

Derrick seems delighted over my response. "The one and the only. So, now that we've gotten that out of the way, I have a question that has been bothering me ever since I laid eyes on you. Why are you here with Alex Harlow? I don't remember hearing anything in the rumor mill about him dating anyone these days."

My mouth opened and closed a few times as my brows dip in thought. I have no idea how to answer that question and after hearing him confirm the ease with which rumors spread, I chose to keep it vague. "Alex and I have worked to-gether. He invited me tonight so I could do some prospect-ing." Hearing the band nearing the end of the song, I threw in a question of my own. "How do you know Alex?"

"We grew up in the same circles. Our families are old friends, and we went to all the same schools as kids."

I let out a high-pitch squeak when Derrick surprises me with a low dip. With my head tilted towards the ground, and the world around me upside down, my eyes latch onto the clipped movements of a pissed-off Alex heading our way. I slap at Derrick's leg as beg him to pull me back up. Alex catches up with us just as I am righted.

With a menacing growl, Alex rips me from Derrick's arms. I stumble against him, my arms gripping his shoulders tightly as my balance is still off from being upside down too long. I swallow hard as I take in his features. I am taken aback by how hard and cold his eyes appear. As he stares down at me, with his expression unreadable, dread fills my belly.

Holy shit...who pissed in his Cheerios?

Pushing me behind him, he faces off with Derrick, who has yet to show any emotion besides amusement. "I hope you enjoyed stealing my date, Derrick. If you were this hard up for company, you should have told me. I could've made a few phone calls on your behalf."

My jaw unhinges at the hostility laced in Alex's words. Besides a slight tick in his jaw, Derrick doesn't seem fazed. "We were having a wonderful time until you showed up. Haven't seen Lexy in a while. How is she doing, Alex?"

My eyes widen at the mention of Lexy. *What does Derrick know about Lexy?* I glance at Alex in time to see some un-named emotion race over his features, but it is gone before

I can figure out what it means. I move to the side so I can get a better look at both men.

"I'm sure Lexy is fine. We don't keep in touch like we used to." Catching my wrist, Alex pulls me back into his side. In an instant, I melted against him. "Sorry to cut our talk short, Derrick, but we have other engagements to attend."

Before Alex can drag me away, Derrick reaches out and takes my free hand. I freeze as he leans down and places a soft kiss on the back of my hand. "Thank you for the dance. It was a pleasure meeting you, Jessica. I hope to see you again soon."

"No, you won't," Alex replies, his jaw set in an uncompromising line. "This is the only warning you're going to get, so listen up and pay attention. Stay away from Jessica. We've been friends long enough for you to know that those who go against me never come out on top. Leave her alone. Don't look in her direction, and don't seek her out." Without another word, Alex tucks me under his arm and ushers me away.

My feet are on autopilot as we move through the room. I can't wrap my head is around what just happened. The more I think about it, the madder I become. I get that not alerting Alex when I left to dance with Derrick was wrong, but if he had been paying attention to me, I wouldn't have had a reason to consider Derrick's offer in the first place. Anger licks at my insides as I come to an abrupt stop. Letting my inner bitch take over, I face off with Alex.

Wrenching my arm from his death grip I curl my hands into fists by my side. "Alex, what in the hell is your problem? We were just dancing." I stare at him with my eyes narrowed.

He stares back.

With a heavy sigh, he finally breaks the standoff and addresses me. "Don't ever walk away without telling me again. You can't imagine the horrible things that went through my head." His voice shakes as he speaks, and for the briefest moment, I feel sorry for my rash behavior. Then Alex continues speaking and all those remorse feelings I had switch back to anger.

"He had a hard-on for you, Jessica. Seeing that jackass' hands on your body pissed me off. I can't believe you let him touch you." He stops talking and runs a hand through his hair. Gritting his teeth, he frowns at me. "We can talk about this later. Carson is bringing the car around. We're leaving." His clipped tone leaves no room for argument. I curb my inner need to argue my point and stay quiet as I give him the time he needs to calm down.

Alex is walking so fast I'm literally stumbling to keep up with him. Running in high heels should be included as a sport in the Olympics. I can assure you, it takes talent and skill to accomplish moving at high-speed in them without breaking an ankle. Unfortunately, those are two things I'm lacking in at the moment. Alex must agree because he abruptly stops, scoops me up in his arms, and continues on without ever missing a beat.

I stare at him in surprise before my anger kicks in, and then I kick frantically and beg to be put down. People all around us are speaking in hushed tones, pointing in our direction, and enjoying the spectacle we are creating.

"Quiet, Jessica," Alex orders softly but sternly. "When we get home, I will give you plenty to squeal about. You can be as loud as you want then. In fact, I hope you are. I love making you scream," he murmurs against my ear. I huff a deep breath but keep quiet as he strides to the waiting limo where Carson stands with the back door held open.

Holy shit!

Chapter Thirteen

Bursting through the front door like a man on a mission, Alex slams the door shut behind us and pins me to it. My breath catches in my throat as my back hits the solid wood of the door. I moan into his mouth as he kisses me. The pressure in my core increases to a relentless throb, beating in time to our ragged breaths. I lean into his body and let out a needy whimper as his solid erection presses into my core. Needing to touch more of him, I make quick work at undressing him.

"You're like my own fucking addiction, baby. You're amazing. I don't think I will ever get enough of you." His words are spoken with a conviction I can't argue with. A knot of emotion builds in my throat, and all I can do is stand there and nod up and down like a crazy person. Luckily Alex seems to understand and doesn't push me for words.

"I don't ever want to see you wrapped up in another man's arms again," he says, trailing kisses down my jaw to my neck.

I nod in agreement. Squeezing my eyes shut, I arch my neck to the side as his lips continue their plunder, nipping at my earlobe and dusting dozens of small kisses above my breasts.

Without warning, I'm spun around, and my hands are placed against the door frame. "Keep them there," Alex commands, and like a good girl, I obey. His velvety voice and the way his body is rubbing against my backside has my sex wet and primed for him. Placing his leg in between mine, he uses it to pry my feet apart.

My heart beats fast as he grasps the zipper of my gown and slowly eases it down, letting my dress fall to the floor before tossing it on a nearby chair. Standing in nothing but my high heels and my birthday suit, the cool air licks at my naked flesh, sending a shiver down my spine.

My hands shake as they cling to the frame with an iron grip. "Keep your hands steady. Don't move them," he demands.

I rest my forehead against the door and pant heavily as anticipation curls deep in my belly. I hold my breath as he gently trails his fingers down my back, over my backside, and down to my dripping sex. I release the moan I was holding in as he sinks two fingers inside me. I'm open and vulnerable as I wait for him to make his next move, never knowing what will come next.

He slides his fingers in and out of me before retreating and running them through my wetness, spreading it around my folds, and soaking my swollen clit. His light caresses are not enough. I buck my hips against his hand as I try and force his fingers back inside me, but being the greedy bastard he is, he pulls back and refuses me any more pleasure than he is willing to give freely.

"Who do you belong to Jessica?" He teases my clit with soft feather-like strokes.

I whimper my displeasure. My mouth goes dry as he bends down and runs his tongue along the apex of my thigh. "Tell me, Jessica. Who do you belong to?"

Oh...my God!

My body is on fire. I try and form the words I know he wants to hear, but my mind has lost the ability to think through my body's need for release. Licking my lips, I push past my arousal and focus on making my vocal cords comply. "You, Alex. I belong to you."

His eyes meet mine, and I marvel at the raw desire staring back at me. Running his hands up my legs, I let out a small moan as his palm cups my mound. "God, you're drenched," he whispers against my skin. The deep rumble of his voice flames my blood. I rest my head against the door as I silently beg him to keep touching me.

As if hearing my wordless plea, Alex plunges two fingers into me. His strokes are slow and steady. I shift my weight as the pleasure builds. My short, rapid breaths fill the room as my climax nears. Moving his hand, he increases his thrusts as his thumb rubs directly over my clit. It's all too much, and yet it is precisely what I need. My body quivers and my back arches as my release rushes over me. My mind blanks as I surrender to the overwhelming feelings assaulting my body from the inside out.

"That's it, baby. Let it all go. Let me feel you," he urges as he continues to milk the last of my orgasm from me.

Standing, he scoops up my wilted body into his strong arms and carries me down the hall to his bedroom. I will never let him know it, but I am thrilled to be in his arms. Not that it would have mattered because I'm pretty sure my jelly legs couldn't have carried me this far on their own.

I glance at him as he lays me down on the bed. My mouth waters as I run my eyes down his perfect body. His cock hangs thick and heavy between his legs. The need to touch him is fierce, but before I get the chance, Alex has my hands in his grasp. Using a tie lying on the bedside table he binds my hands above my head to a slot in the headboard.

I blink in surprise as I test the bonds. They're tight enough to tether me to the bed, but the silk from the tie is soft enough to not hurt me. I've never been restrained during sex before. I can't tell if the hammering of my heart is from nerves or anticipation. Alex molds his hands over my breasts. My nipples pucker as he taunts them with his skilled fingers, tweaking and pulling at them in a way that sends a jolt straight between my legs.

"Let me touch you, Alex," I plead between ragged breaths.

He shakes his head as he looks up at me through his thick lashes. "No, baby. Not right now. Tonight is all about you and the pleasure I want to give you."

Oh boy!

Wanting his lips back on mine, I wrap my ankles around the small of his back and pull him closer until his lips find me once again. The heels of my feet dig into his back as our kissing becomes more aggressive.

He moves his mouth to my ear and whispers. "I like you tied to my bed." His breath against my sensitive skin has me dizzy with lust. "I wish I could keep you here like this all the time."

I snort. "Why, Mr. Harlow? Afraid I will run from you?"

He raises his eyebrows. "More than you know, love." There is a tinge of sadness in his voice that surprises me.

My eyes narrow. "I am trying, Alex. I have given you more than I've given anyone in a long time." I hate how defensive my voice sounds. The moment the words leave my mouth, I wish I could take them back. My emotional baggage is not Alex's fault, and I have no right taking my frustration out on him. I need to sort out my shit out.

Maybe Travis was right. Maybe I am broken.

Alex sighs as he watches me warily. "No more thinking tonight. Just feel. Feel me loving you. Feel how your body responds to me."

Speech has totally eluded me as I stare up into his face. I want nothing more than to please this beautiful man who consumes me. As our eyes meet, he lets out a groan of satisfaction.

His lips curve into a salacious grin as his hand skims through my folds. "I love how wet you get for me. You're so responsive." Positioning himself between my legs, he takes a firm hold of my hips as he places his cock at my opening. With measured movements, he coats the tip of his cock with my wetness before plunging in. With one forceful thrust, he takes me to the hilt.

"Alex!" I bow against my restraints as a heady mixture of pain and pleasure racks my body. Not giving me any time to acclimate to his size, he hammers into me with powerful strokes. My stomach coils as he slides back and forth, flexing his hips, and going deeper with each thrust.

"You feel incredible. Don't stop." I pant as my imminent orgasm builds to a crescendo. I close my eyes and concentrate on feeling him buried deep inside me, filling me, and stretching me in the most delicious way. It's perfect. *He's perfect.*

Grasping my right knee, he hitches it over his shoulder, alternating the angle of his strokes as he continues his brutal momentum. The pleasure coursing through me has my eyes rolling to the back of my head. I can't get enough of him. With each punishing stroke I push back, needing more; the building release threatens to be my undoing.

"You can't leave me, Jessica," he growls low, his dark eyes locking me in place. He kisses me passionately, his tongue claiming and possessing me with a need that has me dizzy and breathless. "Promise me, you won't ever leave me. I need to hear you say it, baby. Promise me, Jessica," he commands, his voice ragged and slightly frantic.

He stills his hips and stares down at me, his eyes pleading with me to agree. I grit my teeth in frustration as I feel my arousal waning. *Oh, hell no!* My heart slams against my chest as the words fly from my mouth. "I promise, Alex. I will never leave you."

With a satisfied grin, he picks his pace back up. I dig my nails into his tie as the pressure in my groin builds to a painful level. I want to tell him I need to come, but the only words I get out between pants and gasps are "Oh fuck," and "Now, please."

"Okay, baby. Let go. Come with me," he shouts, somehow understanding what I was trying to articulate. Doing just as he instructed, I let go.

With my head thrown back, my body arches into his, and I let out a strangled scream as my core detonates in a shattering orgasm that has me seeing white. With a groan of his own, Alex follows me over, losing himself as he groans out incoherent words and promises against my skin.

Spent, Alex collapses against me. We lay together in a tangled heap until our breathing evens out. Leaning up on his side, he reaches up and unties my hands. My arms ache as I lower them to access my wrists. Besides a faint, red ring encircling each of them, everything appears fine. I lay in a daze as Alex pulls me against him, tucking me into his chest as his arms wrap around my waist.

On the cusp of falling asleep, my eyes flicker open to meet his. "Alex, why are you afraid I will leave you?"

His silence unnerves me. I count out the beats of his heart as I wait him out. By the time I get to fifteen, I am close to climbing the walls. I'm afraid that whatever he has to say will change everything. Not able to take anymore, I glance up. His face is grim.

He clears his throat and shifts so we can see each other better. "My past is complicated, and there are parts of my family history that are ugly. It's hard to grow up with lots of money and not have secrets. They seem to go hand in hand," he muses. "There are some things that happened a while back I think you should know about, but I would prefer if we can do it later. You wore me out, and it's nothing that can't wait."

I lick my lips nervously. "That sounds ominous," I murmur. "When are you planning on revealing these secrets to me?"

He closes his eyes and hugs me tighter to him. "Tomorrow, baby. I will tell you all about my whole fucked-up family tomorrow. I promise."

Staring into his sleepy eyes, I nod my agreement. He tucks me back against his chest as he nuzzles his face in my neck. I curl my hands against his chest as I melt into him. After the crazy night and rowdy sex, I am more than ready for sleep.

"Rest, baby," he coaxes, his voice soft and hypnotizing."

I can't find the energy to argue with him as I give into my weighted eyes. With his body wrapped around me like a warm cocoon, I silently send up a little prayer that whatever skeletons Alex plans on letting out of the closet tomorrow is something that I can live with.

I drift off to sleep wondering what tomorrow will bring.

Chapter Fourteen

I wake up with Alex draped over me like a thick, heavy blanket. His warm breath tickles my neck as a light snore escapes his parted lips. Snoring of any kind normally irritates me to no end. I find the sound comparable to nails sliding down a chalkboard, but laying here listening to Alex has the opposite effect on me. His snores are soft and, dare I say, adorable. I rub my tired eyes as my brain tries to sort out everything from the night before. Last night was intense.

Being as stealthy as possible, I carefully pry myself from his grasp and tiptoe to the bathroom. After using the facilities, I wash my hands and sneak a peek in the mirror. I freak at the sight of my tangled hair and raccoon eyes. I resemble a bad replica of the bride of Frankenstein. I hope to hell he didn't see me looking this bad last night.

Using the toiletries Alex bought for me the last time I was here, I comb through my hair and wash the remainder of my makeup off my face. Sneaking back into his room, I grab a large shirt out of his drawer before heading towards the kitchen in search of some coffee. No morning is a good morning without a strong cup of java. I ruffle through several cabinets before finding everything I need. While I wait for it to finish percolating, I busy myself with setting out two cups, spoons, the sugar dispenser, and last but never least, the milk.

As I'm filling our cups, I hear a rustling sound come from the entry way. I smile as I go to investigate. Expecting to find Carson or Alex in the living room, my stomach drops as I come face-to-face with a smug looking Lexy. A moment passes as we both check each other out. I guess you could say we were both summing up the enemy. No matter how you slice it, that is what we are to each other, enemies after the same thing.

I hate to admit it, but Lexy is even prettier up close. Her thick hair rests in perfect waves on her head like real, spun gold, matching the golden hue of her deep tan. I take in a shallow breath as my brain kicks back into gear. *How did she get in here?* No one can access the penthouse elevator without a special security card. I will crush Alex's balls to dust if he gave this bitch access to his personal home.

"Lexy, right?" I keep my voice low as I speak, not wanting to wake Alex until I can work some answers out of our guest.

She scrunches her nose up at me as she speaks. "The one and only. And you are the gullible and naive Jessica."

Unease blossoms in my belly as I absorb her words. *Sticks and stones*, I mentally remind myself. Refusing to appear weak in her presence, I plant my hands on my hips and give her a bored glare. "Alex is still asleep. I think I wore him out last night. Maybe I help you with something?"

"No, I'm good. I came to see you, not Alex." Her tone is sharp as her eyes narrow on me. The way she continues to study me has me on edge. I don't know what Lexy is up to, but I've dealt with girls like her before and whatever she is up to won't be in my benefit. Probably not Alex's either.

A harsh laugh bursts from my lungs. "Lucky me. And to what do I owe the honor of your presence?" My tone is snappy, letting her know that I'm not happy with her intrusion.

She purses her lips and inches closer to me. I want to take a step back, but I stay rooted to my spot. Her next words are my undoing. "I'm curious. Have you enjoyed fucking my husband?"

I blink as a shiver courses down my spine. *Did I hear her correctly?* She called Alex her husband. Not ex-boyfriend but husband. She has to be mistaken. My voice shakes as I speak. "Your husband?" Everything just stops around me. I look away to keep the tears clouding my vision from being seen. There is no way I will crack in front of this bitch.

"Yes, silly girl, my husband. As in till death do us part and all that. Did Alex forget to tell you he was married?" Her face twists with hatred as she continues to speak. "You thought he cared for you, didn't you? How sad. You are nothing but an easy fuck. I generally look past his indiscretions, but he crossed the line parading you in public last night. "

I can practically feel my heart shatter into a million pieces. "He told me you were his ex-girlfriend, not his wife," I answer around the lump taking up residence in my throat.

My mind spins with unanswered questions. When did they get married? Why don't they live together? Do they have an open marriage? Why isn't it public knowledge they are together? Did he ever care for me? How will I survive this?

I glance behind me as Alex comes storming out of his bedroom. The distress and anger is evident in his features as he nears us. Even furious he looks beautiful. I open my mouth to say something, but nothing but a whimper comes out.

"What the hell are you doing here, Lexy?" Stopping beside me Alex's cold, green eyes bore into the little witch. "You promised you wouldn't interfere. I hope you appreciate the shit storm my lawyers will be throwing your way. By the time they are through with you, you won't know what hit you, sweetheart."

Lexy at least has the good sense to look nervous as Alex yells at her. With a vein throbbing in his forehead, and his face flushed red, he looks close to having a stroke. *Good riddance.* The bastard deserves that and so much more. As Alex reaches for me, I duck out his grasp and head back to the bedroom.

I stumble around the room frantically looking under and around furniture until I find my clutch from last night. I rub at my chest swearing that any moment my heart will come crashing through it. The pain is excruciating. Not even Travis had this effect on me.

I can hear the two of them yelling at each other in the other room, but I've become too numb to comprehend what they're saying. Not that I care anymore. I just want to go home and curl up in my bed and cry. Using my cell, I call a cab while snagging a pair of Alex's gym shorts to wear. I leave my shoes, dress, and the necklace he gave me last night spread out on the bed. The thought of keeping anything that came from him makes me feel ill.

When I re-enter the living room, Lexy is gone. My eyes land on Alex, finding him sitting on the sofa with is head resting in his hands. With my mouth set in a firm line, I rush around him, wanting to put as much distance between us as possible. Before I can reach the door, he is on his feet. Grabbing my arm, he spins me around to face him. The anguish marring his beautiful face is not enough to deter the hurt and betrayal coursing through my body.

"Please, listen to me before you walk out that door. You don't have all the facts."

I blink back tears, not yet willing to let them fall. "Are you married to her? Is this a part of the secrets you were planning on talking to me about this morning?"

He dips his head as he leans in. I inhale his familiar scent as it wraps around me like a warm blanket. "Yes," he answers, hanging his head in defeat. "Our marriage is a farce that originated for legal purposes only. We are not in love. The marriage is not about that. Through the years, we've both had other relationships despite being tied together. Our union is not public knowledge and never will be."

"Then why did you do it?"

"My mother had a clause in her will that said I would only gain the controlling shares of the company after I married. The old bat was crazy, but her will was iron-clad. I was desperate at the time. I needed someone who wouldn't screw me over. Lexy is a longtime, family friend with money of her own. It made sense at the time to marry her in name only, to keep my family's company."

My lips part as I stare at him. I'm at a loss for words. This has to be what Derrick was referring to last night with his cryptic remarks about Lexy. What an idiot he must have thought me to be. He probably went home and had a good laugh at my expense

I lick my lips. "Did you ever love her?" Even as I ask the question I want to take it back. I don't want to know the answer. Even if I do need to hear it.

"No. We once tried to make the marriage real but in the end we were only playing house. I've never loved Lexy the way a husband should love his wife. She means nothing to me. I have been working to renegotiate our agreement so I can divorce her. Lexy is fighting me on it. She owns a large portion of shares from my company and is threatening to sell them to my biggest competitor if I dissolve our marriage. My lawyers are working to find a loop hole or something we can use against her."

I'm such a fool. Once again a rich boy has played me. Fool me once, shame on you. Fool me twice shame on me. There will not be a third time.

I take a shaky breath as I lean up and plant a kiss on Alex's cheek. Without another word, I start back toward the front door. I need time to think. Being this close to him, and smelling his familiar, comforting scent, is making it too hard to sort through my feelings.

As I turn the knob, the sound of glass breaking behind stops me dead in my tracks. Glancing behind me, my eyes latch onto the now broken vase scattered across the living room floor. My stomach dips as I catch sight of the tears falling freely down Alex's face.

"You promised you would never leave me," he yells. His eyes are a window to the pain he is feeling. I want to ease his pain, but I can't. He caused this, not me.

He stares at me with an intense concentration. "You said you were mine, Jessica. You can't walk out on us. No one fits you the way I do. We were made for each other."

My hurt turns to anger as I answer him. "I did promise those things, but you also promised not to hurt me. Look how that turned out. I need time to think, Alex. You owe me that. You lied to me more than once. You told me she was only an old girlfriend. I don't know if I can get over that."

"How long?" He asks taking a step towards me. "How much time do you need?"

I shake my head in frustration. "I don't know. There is no time frame for this sort of thing."

With one final glance his way, I walk out the door and shut it soundly behind me. I take the elevator down to where I find my cab waiting at the curb for me. Slipping into the backseat, I am relieved when the driver ignores my hiccupping sobs and endless tears and just drives.

Sadness settles like a bowling ball in the pit of my stomach. I feel truly broken. I always thought Travis broke me years ago, but now I know differently. As much as I cared for Travis, he never had the power to break me. I never loved him enough for him to have that kind of long lasting result on me. Alex can and he did. He still does.

My phone buzzes as we near my home. Swiping the screen, I look down to find a text that has sent.

Alex: I will give you time, but I'm not giving you up. I'm sorry I hurt you and I'll work until the day I die to make it up to you. You're it for me, baby. You are mine as I am yours.

Laying back with my head resting on the cab seat, I swallow down a hoarse cry. I grip my chest as I find it hard to breathe through the searing hurt spreading through my system. My heart pounds hard as a clarity rang true to me.

I'm in love with Alex Harlow. Fuck me sideways but it's true. Somehow, in the mix of everything that has happened, I have fallen in love with him. Holy hell, I am in love with a married man!

What this means for us in the future—if there is a future for us—I have no idea. I guess only time will tell.

To Be Continued in Embracing Him

About the Author

C. Shell resides in the scorching state of Texas with her husband and three lovely daughters. She is passionate about romance novels, especially those featuring a bad boy or alpha male who likes to take charge. When she's not creating fierce and independent characters, she dedicates her time to rescuing dogs in the local community.

Feel free to reach out with any questions, stay updated on her latest releases, and share your thoughts with her.

Visit me at:
http://www.cshellauthor.com
contactme@cshellauthor.com
www.facebook.com/cshellauthor
www.tiktok.com/c.shellauthor

Check out my other Books!

C. Shell - Book Checklist

HARLOW SERIES

- ◯ Beneath Him
- ◯ Embracing Him
- ◯ Completing Him

YOURS SERIES

- ◯ Anonymously Yours
- ◯ Only Yours

CW BOYS SERIES

- ◯ The Beginning
- ◯ Starting Over
- ◯ Tell Me No Lies
- ◯ Happily Ever After

DIRTY LOVE SERIES

- ◯ Dirty Love & Filthy Lies
- ◯ Dirty Love & Sweet Revenge

THE ASSOCIATES

- ◯ Unholy Creations
- ◯ Runes & Embers - Coming Soon

LINK SERIES

- ◯ Weak Link
- ◯ .Second Book - TBA